KALKHAM

DANCE OF PEACOCKS

BOOK 2

VENKATESH NAGARAJAN

KALKHAM

Kalkham is a thrilling mystery series.

It is a journey through time, secrets, and adventure.

Every book brings a new mystery.

For those who love stories, wonder, and

the thrill of the unknown.

KALKHAM SERIES

Books	Availability
Book 1 - The Secret Portal	Available on amazon.com
Book 2 - Dance Of Peacocks	Available on amazon.com
Book 3 and more	Updates on kalkham.com

WWW.KALKHAM.COM

HAVE YOU READ?

Book 1 - The Secret Portal

KALKHAM mystery deepens. Galactic alignment nears. An ancient curse awakens. Dark forces move in secret. A monstrous serpent guards a hidden portal, and Kal's sun-powers emerge. If evil Zhautren returns, there will be no hope for humanity. Destiny has chosen Kal—but is he ready?

WHAT READERS SAY

KALKHAM Book 1 - The Secret Portal has captivated readers with its gripping narrative, immersive storytelling, and mind-bending twists. Here's what readers from around the world have to say about the journey through time, myths, and secrets:

★★★★★ **"5 Stars! Amazing book.**
Will keep you entertained during travel and a delight for readers who have interest in fiction.
— Amazon India Customer

★★★★★ **"Absolutely intriguing!**
The blend of mythology, mystery, and science fiction makes it a must-read. The concept of portals and ancient knowledge is beautifully woven into the story. A fascinating adventure that keeps you hooked till the end!"
— Google Play Books Review

★★★★★ **"Very interesting suspense novel. Too good!"**
"A very interesting novel... It keeps you engaged from start to finish. The narration is so well-paced that you don't feel like pausing even for a moment. That's the level of passion it generates. A must-read!"
— Manasa

⭐⭐⭐⭐⭐ **"Gripping and well-paced! A blend of mystery and adventure."**
"The themes of time, mystery, and ancient wisdom make this book a thrilling read. It kept me thinking long after I finished!"
— Amazon International Review

⭐⭐⭐⭐⭐ **"A thrilling read, especially for mythology lovers!"**
"This book takes you on a journey that is both fascinating and thought-provoking. Looking forward to the next part!"
— Amazon UK Customer

⭐⭐⭐⭐⭐ **"Couldn't put it down!"**
"A page-turner with a unique storyline. The writing is immersive, and the suspense keeps building. Highly recommended!"
— Google Play Books Review

⭐⭐⭐⭐☆ **"The novel is very good and creates curiosity as we proceed."**
"The eagerness to continue reading leads to completion fast. :) Loved it!"
— Rashmi

⭐⭐⭐⭐☆ **"Amazing book. Great for travel reading!"**
"A delight for readers who love fiction and mythology. Looking forward to the next part!"
— Amazon Customer

★★★★☆ **"A fascinating read that kept me hooked from start to finish."**
"The storytelling is immersive, and the concept is unique. Definitely recommended for fiction lovers!"
— Amazon India Customer

★★★★★ **"Great Read..!!"**
"Amazing Novel!! The author's imagination and storytelling capability are truly commendable. This book is a must-read for all fiction lovers. I thoroughly enjoyed reading it and am eagerly waiting for the next book."
— Jeena

★★★★★ **"Five Stars!"**
"Awesome book... Wonderful imagination! Waiting eagerly for the continued part... Hope we get that soon to be occupied!" — Sushma, Amazon India

★★★★★ **"A very beautiful story with great narration!"**
"Hats off to the imagination of the author. The storytelling is captivating and keeps you engaged throughout!"
— Anonymous Mr. S, Amazon India

★★★★★ **"Great book!!"**
"An interesting and intriguing story! Hats off to the author for the story... It took my imagination to the next level. Eagerly waiting for the next book to see where the story goes."
— Amazon India Customer

📖 **Have you read the KALKHAM mystery books?**

Leave your review on Amazon, or your preferred platform.

BOOK 1 - THE SECRET PORTAL

Print Edition	Ebook Edition
Amazon India UK, Others	Kindle
Flipkart	Google Play
NotionPress	Scribd
	Kobo

AVAILABLE WORLDWIDE

Dedicated to Bharathavarsha,
the land of eternal spiritual wealth.

Even the air I breathe is not mine,
nor is the sky, nor is the fire in spine.
All I can own is — 'Time'.

To own Time,
all that I have is — 'Now'.

ACKNOWLEDGMENTS

Dear Reader,

I wrote this story only for you. A timeless tale imprinted in the DNA of our worlds. How could I reach out a message to you alone? Right from situations that surround us, sounds that shield us, and the sky that covers us, all serve a purpose.

Powerful worldly affairs and pursuits can keep you away from some secrets forever. Hence, I have sent you an encrypted message through these books. Until the last word, the message is hidden.

One day, you will be ready, old enough to start reading stories again. You would still be swimming along waves of memories, too tired to iron the wrinkles on your skin. Time may continue to weave colors, but I shall still be your affectionate KALKHAM.

Before you start reading this book, let's take a moment to remember the sun, the ever glowing principle who guides our journey from darkness to light.

My humble thanks and respects to teachers, almighty and well-wishers.

Lovingly,
Venkatesh Nagarajan

PROLOGUE

Story so far...

A legendary treasure hunt in Egypt has come to a terrifying halt—stopped by an ancient and deadly curse. Ten brilliant scientists have mysteriously fallen into a deep coma, and the only way to revive them is with an ancient secret — the Lilbido. But just as hope appears, the key to their survival is stolen by mysterious impostors who vanish without a trace.

Determined to unravel the mystery, Kalyan embarks on a perilous journey to find Babaji, who holds the answers. Along the way, he is drawn into a hidden tribal civilization, where an astonishing revelation shakes his identity—they believe he is the incarnation of their Sun God. Destiny takes a shocking turn when he gains possession of the Quoltha, an ancient gemstone of immense power.

A galactic alignment looms, threatening to awaken a force the world has long forgotten—Zhautren, the one who should never return. The modern world carries on, blind to the dark forces rising beneath its feet.

Then, a dream—so vivid, so otherworldly—pierces through Kalyan's soul, delivering an urgent message.
Something beyond the prophecy awaits the modern world!
KALKHAM mystery deepens. What awaits us at the end of the book is not just an ordinary tale but an immersive experience.

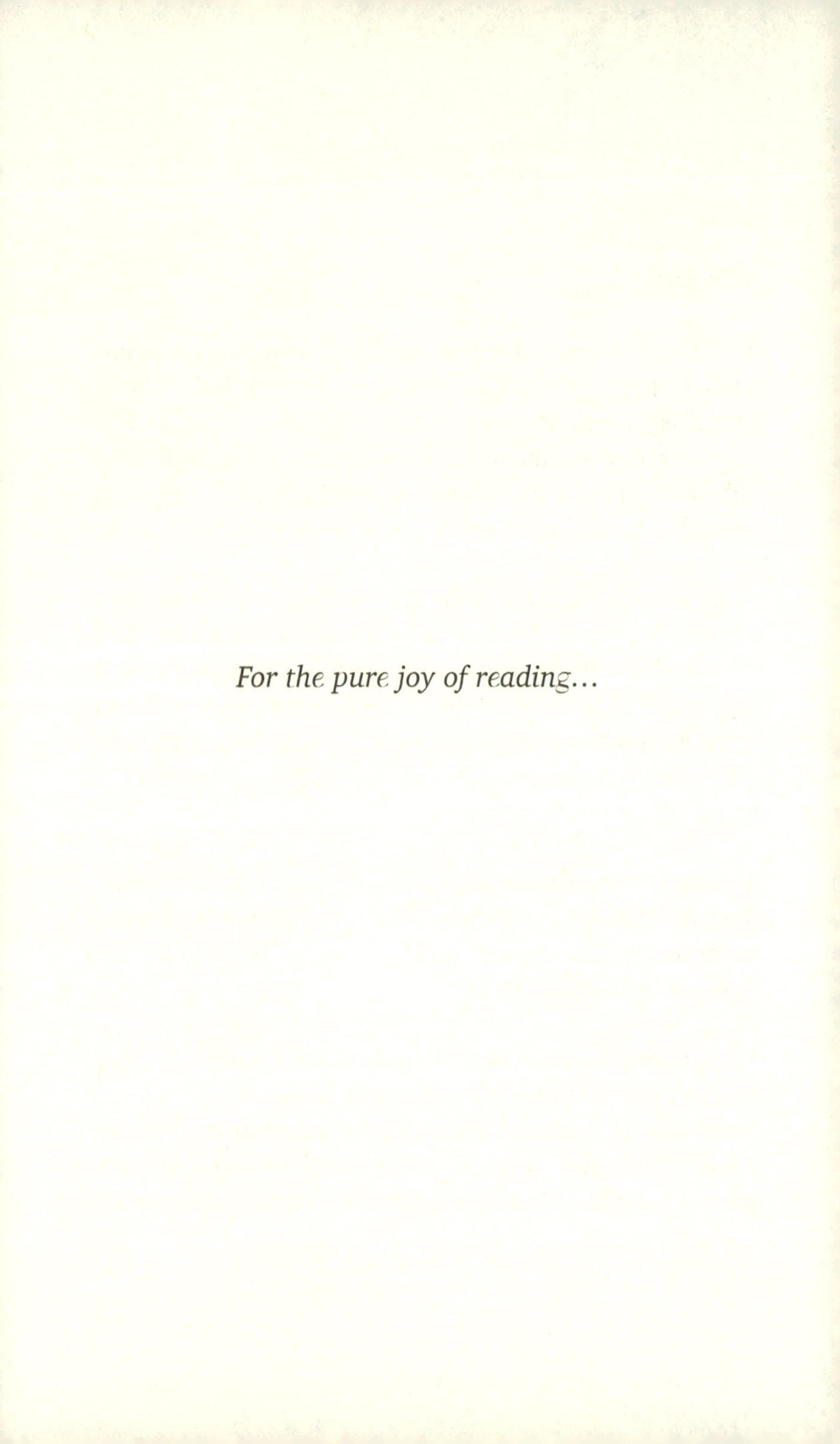

For the pure joy of reading…

CONTENTS

CHAPTER 1

SOMETHING IS NOT RIGHT

"There are always signs… right before it begins."

"Oh, not again!" sighed Tony, staring at his AI robot. The robot's sensor wasn't connecting to his supercomputer and the beeping grew louder, demanding his attention. He got up from his desk to attend to it.

Tony Lee was a prodigy—sharp-minded, intensely focused, and always buried in research papers or complex simulations. With his round glasses perched on his nose and an ever-serious expression, he had the unmistakable look of a genius lost in thought.

At just 24, he had already earned the position of Project Lead at the Earth Research & Monitoring Division (ERMD), a top-secret government institute dedicated to studying Earth's tectonic movements, solar impacts, and deep mineral structures. His journey to ERMD had been nothing short of remarkable. He had graduated at the top of his class from China's highest-ranked university, setting records with his exceptional grades.

His unmatched IQ made him a legend among professors and researchers, many of whom believed he was destined for something far greater than ordinary scientific work.

But Tony had little interest in fame—his passion lay in research, in uncovering the hidden truths of the Earth's ever-changing dynamics.

His skills and dedication earned him the unwavering trust of Mr. Chiam Agung, the powerful and highly influential political figure who oversaw ERMD's confidential projects.

Mr. Chi saw in Tony not just brilliance, but reliability—an asset that could be trusted with the kind of information that never reached the public eye.

The ERMD team operated in complete secrecy; their findings reported only to Mr. Chi, who had the final say on what the world needed to know.

Tony rarely questioned the weight of the classified knowledge he handled. His mind was always fixed on the next discovery, the next anomaly, the next unexplained phenomenon that could reshape humanity's understanding of Earth. But deep down, he knew—something about their latest research didn't add up. And soon, that realization would change everything.

"What happened now?" Lisha asked, as Tony abruptly stood up, pushing his chair back.

Lisha was Tony's girlfriend. They had met during their first year at university, both drawn to the world of research and discovery. He was the reserved genius, always buried in books and calculations, while she was the sharp-witted problem solver who challenged every theory he believed in.

Their late-night study sessions turned into endless debates, and somewhere between equations and coffee-fueled research papers, they had fallen in love.

Lisha admired Tony's brilliance, the way his mind worked faster than anyone else's, while he found himself captivated by her determination and curiosity. By the time they graduated, their bond had grown stronger—not just as partners in love, but as a team driven by the same purpose.

Lisha leaned against Tony's desk, arms crossed, watching him with a mix of curiosity and concern. "What happened now?" she asked again.

Without answering, he rushed toward the AI robot standing by the major terminal. Its sensor light flickered red, signaling a connection failure. He adjusted his round glasses and crouched down, inspecting the loose connection.

"The sensor got disconnected from the supercomputer," he muttered.

Lisha sighed. "Again? That's the third time this week."

Tony nodded and reconnected the tiny cables with steady hands. "Something's not right, Lisha," he said, standing up and pulling up satellite data on his screen. "For the last three days, the Earth's surrounding layers haven't been showing normal readings. It's like something is interfering—tampering with the natural signals."

Lisha stepped closer, her brows furrowed. "Tampering? With the Earth's layers? That's... insane. By who?"

Tony exhaled, frustrated. "That's what I'm trying to figure out. I programmed the AI bot to read signal variations between satellite G7112 and satellite G8892. One satellite is in the northern hemisphere, and the other is at the exact opposite end of the Earth. If there was an anomaly, comparing both data sets would expose it."

"And?" Lisha asked, her voice tense.

Tony pointed to the screen. "The AI was supposed to gather and analyze the data for a full 16-hour cycle. But just when I was about to review the results, the sensor beeped— connection failed."

Lisha's eyes widened. "Wait... does that mean—"

"All the data is lost," Tony finished, slamming his fist on the desk. "Sixteen hours of critical work, gone."

Lisha placed a hand on his shoulder. "Tony… if someone doesn't want us to see that data, that means we're onto something."

Tony's fingers hovered over the keyboard. He stared at the blinking screen, his mind racing.

"Exactly," he whispered.

"There is only one option left. I'll connect this to your palm chip. In case this disconnects itself again, this will then auto-route and capture all recordings in offline mode making the data accessible only after 24 hours. At least we will have the recordings. We can run the analytics later on." He said.

"Fine," Lisha agreed, pinching her finger to confirm access to the tiny chip implanted in her palm.

Suddenly the phone rang, breaking the tense atmosphere. Lisha grabbed it. It was from Mr. Chi. "Yes, Mr. Chi?" she answered while putting him on speaker.

"Both of you, leave immediately. A private jet is waiting at the restricted airbase. Come to Shillong— It's protocol-22, this is classified." His voice was sharp.

"Protocol-22? What happened, Mr. Chi?" asked Tony, his face full of shock as his eyebrows drew together.

"Well, there have been some strange findings from India. I'm sitting next to Dr. Upen. We need help in reviving the scientists from coma. Do not waste time, we finally got the black rose extract," he said.

Tony and Lisha exchanged glances. Lisha nodded - "Wow, that's great news!"

"See you soon then!" His voice was urgent as he disconnected the call.

"Finally, Dr. Upen has done it again. He always finds a way to save the world from trouble." Tony said.

"But, isn't it strange? Mr. Chi said Protocol-22 instead of Protocol-3. Right?" asked Lisha in surprise.

"That means it's very urgent. Let's hurry. I'll grab the specimen from the freezer. You get the pen drive and the blue file," said Tony. His mind was racing.

"You might be rushing, Tony, but my instincts are telling me something isn't right." said Lisha as she took the blue file and pen drive from the 'TOP SECRET' shelf as per Protocol-22.

Within a minute, they were out of the lab.
"Beep… Beep…" The AI robot beeped again.
Someone was tampering with the Earth's natural signals—again.

❖

CHAPTER 2

TICK TOCK

"Bad people use your kindness against you."

A few hours later, Tony and Lisha arrived at a secluded science laboratory on the remote outskirts of Shillong. The facility, hidden from the outside world, operated under the highest levels of confidentiality.

"But that day, strangely, there were no security guards in sight — only towering, sleek entry portals equipped with advanced biometric scanners. Someone had apparently disabled them for easy access to the high-tech compound.

"Maybe since Mr. Chi said it was urgent on the call, that's why they were disabled," thought Tony."

As they reached the designated room, the sleek sliding door parted soundlessly, revealing Dr. Upen in deep discussion with Mr. Chi and all other world leaders seated in a conference.

Dr. Upen gestured toward a set of digital panels, explaining his breakthrough—an extract derived from black roses, capable of reviving a person from a deep coma.

Suddenly, a digital voice in the room announced their arrival: "Guests are here."

Mr. Chi turned toward them. His expressions shifting from focus to acknowledgment. With a nod, he welcomed the two into their world of classified research and hidden truths, collecting the specimen from Tony and the pen drive from Lisha.

Dr. Upen took a deep breath, his gaze sweeping across the room filled with world leaders, their faces etched with anticipation.

He stepped forward, holding up a small vial containing a shimmering, dark liquid. The weight of the moment pressed upon him as he spoke with urgency.

"This is it… the extract from black roses," he declared, his voice firm.

"With this, I present hope. Mr. President of Egypt, this extract can revive your ten scientists who have been in a coma for the last few days." He gestured toward his assistants, Jenny and Nyra, who carefully stepped forward, handing the vial to the Egyptian president with solemn precision.

A murmur spread through the room, eyes widening in disbelief and curiosity. Sensing their unspoken questions, Dr. Upen continued, "I know this seems like a miracle, but this knowledge is ancient. It was first introduced to me in my younger days by a wise man—Babaji, the grandfather of my dear friend Kalyan."

His eyes flickered with memory. "In the remote hills of South India, Babaji taught me the science behind this extract. It is not just a medicine—it is a fusion of nature's deepest secrets and human will."

The leaders exchanged glances, some skeptical, others intrigued. The air in the room grew heavier as they awaited the revelation.

"Can I please see that Mr President?" asked Mr. Chi.

"Of course!" The president passed the extract.

The Egyptian president expressed deep gratitude, his voice filled with relief. For the first time, there was hope to revive the ten scientists lost to the mysterious coma during the Project Arizona treasure expedition. He explained how difficult the issue had become and now finally he had some relief. The leaders in the room murmured amongst themselves, processing the gravity of what had just been presented.

There was a pause in the room as it slowly came to settle down. Suddenly, Lisha's palm made a low sound beep. Dr. Upen was sharp. He quickly knew that the sound he heard was not any from his laboratory. He stared at her for a moment.

Tony and Lisha exchanged glances. "Should we tell Mr. Chi that someone is tampering with the earth signals?" She whispered.

"No." Tony said to Lisha by moving his lips. "Mute it" he hinted her by closing his ears. They both looked at Mr. Chi, who was clearly busy setting up his radar scanner device waiting for the pen drive programs to boot up the specimen.

But since Dr. Upen was still staring at her wondering where that beep sound originated, Tony smiled and covered it up by coughing continuously to get his attention.

Just before Dr. Upen could check further, a voice from a far seat interrupted the tense silence.

"Before we move forward, I have a question, Dr. Upen"
This voice sounded familiar to Dr. Upen. He turned around to confirm.

It was Jorthan, who had once been his colleague, a fellow researcher. But rivalry had poisoned their relationship. Long ago, when Dr. Upen refused to share the black rose extract formula, Jorthan had taken it as a personal insult. From that day, he vowed to overshadow Dr. Upen's legacy, even if it meant destroying his reputation.

Dr. Upen had tried to forget about him, but now, here he was, among the world's most powerful leaders. And he was about to strike.

Jorthan walked up and now took a seat next to the president of Egypt and leaned forward with a knowing smirk. His presence and having sided with the president of Egypt, made Dr. Upen uneasy.

Jorthan's sharp eyes gleamed as he spoke. "Dr. Upen, we all admire your scientific contributions," he began, his tone dripping with false admiration. "But tell us—how do we know this extract is safe? You claim it can revive people from a coma, but where is the proof?"

A murmur spread across the room. Dr. Upen hesitated. His mind raced as he knew Jorthan was deliberately cornering him, forcing him to reveal more than he intended.

"The formula is confidential," Dr. Upen said carefully. "We have limited time and a limited quantity of the extract. The focus should be on saving lives, not debating its secrecy."

Jorthan chuckled, shaking his head. "Ah, but that's exactly the problem, isn't it?" His voice grew louder. "This is an untested substance. We have no medical records and no case studies.

What if one or more of these scientists develop severe side effects? Or worse—what if they die?"

A hush fell over the room. Two world leaders, exchanging glances, nodded in agreement.

"He has a point," the Chancellor of Germany said. "Dr. Upen, this extract is unknown to modern medicine. We cannot risk our best minds without guarantees."

"Yes," another leader added. "If this fails, or if there are unforeseen consequences, who will be responsible?"

Dr. Upen's pulse quickened. He had never doubted the extract's effectiveness, but now, under the weight of scrutiny, his fears surfaced.

Jorthan pressed on, his voice sharp. "If your research is so solid, then prove it. Reveal the formula."

Dr. Upen clenched his fists. This was Jorthan's true goal all along—to strip him of his discovery, to force him into a position where he had no choice but to disclose what he had spent years perfecting.

For the first time, Dr. Upen felt cornered. He could see where this was heading. He turned to Jorthan with a measured but firm voice.

"Jorthan, you wanted this formula years ago, and even now, you are still after it. Why?" His gaze bore into Jorthan, searching for the truth in his words. "Is it worth risking the lives of those ten brilliant scientists just to satisfy your grudge against me? Let go of the past. This is not the time to create doubts."

Jorthan, unfazed, smirked mischievously. He had anticipated this response. With deliberate precision, he shifted his gaze toward the President of Egypt, his eyes carrying an unspoken message.

The President, catching the silent exchange, exhaled deeply before addressing Dr. Upen. His voice was calm, but laced with disappointment.

"Dr. Upen," he began, "you gave us hope with this so-called cure. But what you never told us is that this extract is not medically approved. Now, after bringing together world leaders, making us travel here—off the record, without security, without any official documentation—you suddenly claim that your formula is too 'confidential' to be shared?"

His expression hardened, his next words cutting through the tension.

"You have been honored and celebrated. Science and the people have trusted you. You are a Nobel laureate. And now you expect us to accept whatever you say?" His tone dropped into something colder, more resolute.

The room remained heavy with silence as Dr. Upen closed his eyes for a brief moment, his thoughts drifting back to the remote hills of South India, recalling the time spent with Babaji.

He could still hear Babaji's voice—calm, yet firm.
"This knowledge is sacred. It is not to be written, nor spoken to unworthy ears. The extract is not just science—it is nature's rarest secret. It must never fall into the wrong hands."

He knew he couldn't reveal the formula. The only way forward was to prove its power. Dr. Upen opened his eyes after this brief moment. His sharp eyes caught something unusual about Jorthan.

Every time he refused to share the formula, Jorthan subtly glanced at his watch and pressed his right ear, as if he were receiving signals or tracking something. It wasn't a nervous habit—it was calculated.

His watch gleamed faintly, displaying something Dr. Upen couldn't quite decipher. Was he reading emotional responses? Was he tracking stress levels?

Dr. Upen was also surprised that the president of Egypt had suddenly flipped his stance on the extract. Just a few minutes ago, he was thankful. But after Jorthan came in, he changed his tone and took a different stance. Something was not right.

Dr. Upen's patience snapped. His voice cut through the air, filled with anger and suspicion. "Jorthan! You're constantly looking at your watch and pressing your ear. What have you been up to?" His eyes burned into Jorthan, demanding an answer.

Then, shifting his gaze to the President of Egypt, his tone grew more resolute. "There is no other option left, Mr. President. The deepest secrets of nature are not meant to be exposed."

"Especially not in the presence of someone I do not trust." He turned his gaze back to Jorthan, his suspicion solidifying.

"Tick-tock, tick-tock," said Jorthan loudly, looking at his watch. "People invented the watch to tell time, but we have changed its purpose. We use it for other readings now…" he said in a serious pitch realizing that he couldn't trick Dr. Upen for long.

Jorthan unfazed, looked at his watch one last time. He was tracking Dr. Upen's mental readings by his watch. A small flicker appeared on the screen—a signal. He smirked.

Dr. Upen had mentally decided that, no matter the pressure, he would never reveal the formula. That was all Jorthan needed to confirm.

With a slow, deliberate motion, he rose from his seat. Before anyone could react, his hand darted toward the table, snatching the lone vial of black rose extract from Mr. Chi.

Holding it high above his head, he looked directly at Dr. Upen, his eyes glinting with triumph. "How can you say there is no other way, Dr. Upen?" Jorthan's voice rang through the silent room.

"There is still one more way." Has said holding the extract raising his hand in the air.

Dr. Upen with eyes widened realized what he was up to. "Jorthan…… Nooooo…." He shouted.

And before anyone could stop him—Jorthan dropped the bottle on the hard floor.

The fate of the black rose extract—of the ten scientists, of everything—was gone in an instant.

❖

CHAPTER 3

BIG TRAP

"Knowledge is beautiful until it becomes destructive."

The world leaders shot up from their seats, their faces filled with shock and rage. Some slammed their hands on the table, others looked around in panic. The only cure—destroyed.

Dr. Upen's eyes burned with anger. He took a step forward, fists clenched. "Jorthan, you destroyed the only cure. Why did you do this?" he asked, his voice sharp and steady.

Jorthan didn't answer right away. Instead, he threw his head back and laughed—a cruel, mocking laugh.

"Revenge," he said, smirking. He lifted his boot and crushed the broken glass even further, grinding it into dust. "Now it's gone forever," he said, his voice dripping with satisfaction.

Jorthan smirked, folding his arms. "You always had everything, didn't you, Upen?" His voice dripped with bitterness. "Back when we worked together, you were always one step ahead—your inventions, your discoveries, always changing the world for the better. And me? No matter how hard I tried, no one cared. My projects were ignored, and my funding was denied. You stole the limelight every single time."

Dr. Upen's jaw tightened, his eyes fixed on Jorthan.

"I thought of being your friend once," Jorthan continued, shaking his head. "But you were never inviting. Always too busy in your own world, never once looking back at those you left behind." He let out a cold chuckle.

"Do you remember the time I asked how you came out of your coma? You refused to tell me. You kept your secret to yourself not even leaving a trace of it on papers knowing I would look for it."

Jorthan stepped closer, lowering his voice. "So I went looking for my answers. One night, I travelled to the caves of Agung. And there… I found something beyond imagination."

His eyes darkened as he spoke. "A voice called to me…"

"Something ancient…"

"Something not from this world…"

"And then… I met Q." Jorthan paused.

"Met who?" Dr. Upen demanded.

Jorthan grinned. "An alien named 'Q'."

"An ALIEN —?" asked Dr. Upen in utter shock.

"Yes, an alien" confirmed Jorthan.

Jorthan's eyes gleamed with twisted pride. "Q made me an offer that night," he said. "It saw the fire in me—the hunger for power, for revenge. And in return for my loyalty, it gave me something far greater than recognition." He raised his wrist, tapping the sleek black watch strapped to his wrist.

"This," he said, his voice filled with arrogance, "is just one of the gifts Q has given me. A technology far beyond human understanding. With this, I can control minds." He glanced at the world leaders in the room. "There isn't a single world leader here who isn't under my control."

The leaders stirred, some gripping the arms of their chairs, others glancing at one another with growing unease.

Jorthan smirked. "But that's not all. Q also taught me how to read brain impulses." Tapping the sleek surface of his watch.

"You see, Upen, this little device isn't just tick-tock, tick-tock." He winked.

"It tracks your brain signals—every spike of fear, every hesitation. I've been watching it closely with every answer you gave." He chuckled, tilting his head.

"I was hoping you'd crack under pressure, that you'd slip up and reveal the formula. But no… you stayed firm."

His smile faded into a scowl as he glanced at the shattered extract on the floor. "That's why I had to do this."

"Now that the only trace of the extract is gone, to save your reputation, Upen, you will make a new one… right? So, you will have to put out the formula, of course. Hahaha," he laughed.

Grinding the broken pieces under his heel, he leaned in closer. "But make no mistake, Upen—I am adamant. I want that secret formula, at any cost."

Dr. Upen's fists tightened as he held his ground.
"Why do you think I will do it for you? The world leaders here will condemn your actions and put you in prison. There will be consequences for this Jorthan." Dr. Upen argued.

"Oh, so you're threatening me, Upen?" he asked. "And the world leaders assembled here condemning me? …Hahaha." He laughed out loud.

All the world leaders were shocked at his words.

He became serious, pressing a button on his watch. "Upen, I will now show you what I'm truly capable of. I will force you to reveal the formula. And knowing you, the so-called 'child of science' born for the people, you won't stand by and watch humanity fall. You'll do it for them."

Jorthan lifted his wrist and spoke into his watch, his voice cold and commanding. "Activate the mind control protocol. All world leaders assembled here—listen to my commands. Your minds are under my control now."

The room fell silent for a moment.

Then, one by one, the world leaders stiffened.

Their eyes glazed over, their expressions vacant.

Slowly, in eerie synchronization, they stood up from their seats, their movements unnaturally rigid.

Dr. Upen, Tony, Lisha, Jenny and Nyra stood frozen, watching in horror. Unlike the leaders, they remained unaffected— Jorthan's control was only over those in positions of power.

Then, the room echoed with a chilling, unified voice.
"Yes, Master. What can we do for you?"

Dr. Upen's breath hitched. "What… what is happening?" he whispered. "This is unbelievable."

Dr. Upen's stomach clenched. He had seen Jorthan's obsession before, his hunger for recognition, his endless grudge. But now, fueled by something far beyond human reach, Jorthan had become truly dangerous.

A memory flashed in his mind—a lecture he had once given his students on suprasonic energy, the very force that keeps planets in their orbits, an energy released by the sun itself. It was a power beyond human reach, a force of nature, a force accessible on earth. But somehow, Jorthan had tapped into it... with nothing more than a simple watch.

His mind raced with a hundred questions. How had Jorthan achieved this? How could he harness the energy of the cosmos to manipulate the minds of world leaders?

Jorthan watched Dr. Upen's stunned expression with satisfaction. "Now," he said, his voice dripping with arrogance, "before I expand this control over every human on Earth, I ask you one last time—will you submit your formula?"

Dr. Upen stared at him, his heart pounding.

Jorthan leaned in, his grin widening. "You see, Upen, I've done more than just tap into the Earth's signals. I've harnessed suprasonic energy itself. It charges my ultra mind-controlling device—the suprasonic device. This watch," he lifted his wrist, "is only a prototype. It lets me control minds for a few minutes at a time."

Lisha and Tony now realized it was Jorthan behind tampering with the earth's signals.

Then, his voice darkened. "But my master, Q… he's built something far greater. A massive device capable of controlling every human on Earth. And it will be unleashed on the upcoming galactic alignment."

The words 'galactic alignment' sent a shiver down Dr. Upen's spine. Nyra had warned him about Zhautren's prophecy. That meant the prophecy was not a mere myth. He had spent his life studying the cosmos, but now, for the first time, he feared it. He realized the grave truth - the raw power of technology… in the wrong hands — dangerous!

Dr. Upen frowned. "I don't believe you. Why would you side with a being that wants to destroy the very world you wish to control?"

Jorthan chuckled, shaking his head. "You always were the smart one, Upen. But this time, you don't see the full picture." His eyes gleamed with a dangerous glow. "Q's plans are far bigger than anything you can imagine. And the best part? No one—not one human—knows what's coming." He laughed.

"What do you mean? You're human, and why do you pride yourself on saying that no human knows?" Dr. Upen laughed to tease his arrogance.

Jorthan laughed loudly in return but chose not to answer.

Did that mean he was not a human? Was he an alien too? Doubts grew in Dr. Upen's mind.

Jorthan threw his head back and laughed. "Hahaha… You'll know soon, Upen," he sneered.

"It's time to take you somewhere," Jorthan said.

Then, with a swift motion, he pressed a command on his watch. "Initiate landing. Bring the ship here."

A mechanical voice from the device confirmed, "Command received," indicating that the UFO landing was in progress.

Suddenly within minutes, a deep, vibrating hum filled the air. The ground beneath them trembled. The walls of the building shook as if caught in an invisible force.

Lisha's palm chip beeped furiously. Earth's signals were heavily tampered with. She and Tony exchanged glances, their eyes widening in realization.

From the very beginning, something had been interfering with their readings—something unnatural, something they couldn't explain. Now, the final piece of the puzzle clicked into place. It was Jorthan's watch all along. The mysterious distortions in Earth's signals, the anomalies they had detected for the last three days, all of it… was caused by him.

"Stop this madness!" Tony thundered, turning toward Jorthan. "How could you even think of tapping into science for such a purpose? This is not just unethical—it's an insult to science itself! To humanity!"

Dr. Upen, however, was still in the dark. His mind raced with possible escape plans, but he knew that Jorthan's watch could track even the slightest impulse in his brain. If he even thought about running, he'd give himself away. He forced himself to stay calm, suppressing his thoughts as best as he could.

Outside, the UFO loomed, its metallic body pulsing with an eerie glow in the sky.

Jorthan turned to the room. "Everyone! Move!"

The world leaders responded in unison, their voices eerily robotic. "Yes, Master…"

Like lifeless puppets, they stepped forward, one by one, walking toward the spacecraft, their expressions blank, their eyes hollow.

Dr. Upen, Tony, Lisha, and Mr. Chi followed behind, their steps hesitant. Jorthan stayed close behind them, a sinister grin on his face, pointing a sleek black gun at their backs.

"It's now time for my boss, Q, to decide your fates," he said, laughing maniacally. The sound of his laughter echoed through the air.

Dr. Upen's mind tried to process what was happening. First, the world's best scientists had fallen into a coma. Now, the leaders of the world were trapped.

"Something is connected. This is indeed a big trap." Dr. Upen thought.

CHAPTER 4

ALIEN 'Q'

"Source of disturbance is sometimes just around you."

The UFO hovered silently in the sky, its surface shimmering like liquid metal, reflecting the eerie glow of the lab building's floodlights. A low hum vibrated through the air, intensifying as the hatch slid open. Jorthan motioned with his gun, his expression devoid of mercy.

"Move!" he commanded coldly.

One by one, the world leaders, still under his mind control, walked forward in perfect synchronization. Their eyes were vacant, their steps eerily robotic.

Dr. Upen, Tony, Lisha, Jenny and Nyra hesitated, their instincts screaming at them to resist. But with Jorthan's gun pointed at their backs, there was no choice.

The group stepped inside, the interior of the UFO glowing with an unnatural luminescence. Mr. Chi was the last to enter. The hatch sealed shut behind him, and the ship lifted off with an almost imperceptible motion—smooth, swift, and unnervingly silent.

Minutes passed. Or was it hours? Inside the craft, there were no windows, no sense of time or direction. The only sound was the rhythmic hum of alien technology, vibrating beneath their feet.

They exchanged nervous glances but dared not speak.

Finally, the ship slowed. A faint hiss signaled the release of pressurized air as the doors slid open, revealing an enormous underground laboratory.

The walls pulsed with veins of glowing green energy, and countless metallic consoles lined the space, covered with holographic displays filled with symbols no human had ever seen. The ceiling stretched high, vanishing into shadows, with floating platforms and walkways connecting different sections of the lab. It was unlike anything Dr. Upen had ever seen.

Inside, the air was thick with an unnatural hum, the walls glowing with shifting alien symbols.

Tony, despite the tense situation, couldn't help but observe the advanced technology surrounding them—floating holograms, strange energy tubes, and machinery running on unknown power sources. They barely had time to register it.

The next doors slid open to reveal a gigantic laboratory filled with towering machines and glass chambers containing creatures and humanoid figures in various stages of transformation. The sight was both fascinating and horrifying.

Dr. Upen turned to Jorthan. "Where are we?"

Jorthan stepped forward, his voice brimming with satisfaction. "Welcome to Q's laboratory, the place where the future of Earth is being rewritten. This is where it all begins." He gestured broadly.

Lisha's eyes narrowed. "Future? You mean destruction?"

Jorthan chuckled. "Oh no, dear Lisha. Not destruction—control. A world where humans will beg for their fate."

Tony stared at a humanoid figure inside a containment chamber. "What is this doing here?"

Dr. Upen's breath caught as he saw something truly terrifying.

On a raised platform in the centre of the room, an alien—sleek, humanoid, but unmistakably otherworldly—stood inside a cylindrical chamber. Before their very eyes, the creature's form began to shift, morphing, twisting... until it took the appearance of a human man.

Jorthan smirked. "Simple. We are making sure that human minds no longer belong to themselves."

Jenny stepped forward, horrified. "That's monstrous!"

Jorthan leaned in. "Monstrous? Or necessary? Imagine a world where no one rebels, no one questions, no one suffers. All will follow Q's will."

"This is just another template used to clone humans," Jorthan said pointing to an adjacent holographic chamber and pushed a lever to show them how it worked.

The chamber's doors opened, and the transformed being floated out, weightless, guided by an unseen force. A launchpad-like station absorbed it, displaying a map of the Earth with blinking markers.

Dr. Upen's voice was hoarse. "What...? What are you doing here, Jorthan? How is this possible?"

Jorthan chuckled. "Ah, Upen, always so curious. The real question is: why haven't you asked how I gained such intelligence?"

Jorthan intentionally was demonstrating the capabilities of the quantum technologies so as to scare Dr. Upen and force him to submit the formula.

Before anyone could respond, Jorthan pressed his fingers to his ear. A faint clicking sound echoed, followed by a grotesque sight—his scalp shifted, revealing the back of his head. Half-human, half-reptilian nerves intertwined with metallic chips, glowing faintly with an eerie light.

Jenny gasped. Tony took a step back. Even Dr. Upen struggled to keep his composure.

Jorthan smirked. "Now you see. This is evolutionary progress, my dear friends. A perfect fusion of man, reptile, and machine."

Lisha stole a glance at Mr. Chi, expecting a reaction, but he remained silent, his face unreadable. Something about his stillness unnerved her.

Tony found his voice. "This... this is beyond cybernetics. These enhancements—how do they even function? Your neural pathways, your consciousness... should've been overwritten by the machine. How are you still in control?"

Jorthan tilted his head, amused. "Control, Tony? That's the word you're focusing on? That's the very essence of Q's plan." His grin widened. "Control. Absolute and undeniable. Over minds. Over bodies. Over life itself."

Dr. Upen's mind raced. "And to what end, Jorthan? What does Q want? World domination? I don't believe it. This grand power hides something very dangerous, something very big. What's his true agenda?"

Jorthan sighed, "You are right Upen!"

"Q doesn't want to rule humans, He wants to redefine their existence. To reshape them into something that will beg for its own survival. And ultimately… to seek him as their god."

A chilling silence filled the room.

Jorthan continued, pacing slowly.

"Death is the greatest fear of mankind. We fear it, resist it, and try to prolong life by every means possible. But what if death itself was no longer in your hands? What if it belonged to him?" He gestured at the vast network of machines around them.

"What if humans lived in such terror, in such oppression, that the only way out was to ask for death? And only one entity could grant it?" His eyes gleamed.

"That, my dear Upen, is true power. And now, this power lies with Q," he finished.

"Power lies with 'Q'?" asked Dr. Upen puzzled. "What do you mean? Do you mean alien 'Q' can now control anyone from dying?"

Lisha felt an icy chill crawl down her spine. But her attention kept drifting to Mr. Chi. He was too quiet. Too still. Almost as if… he wasn't fully there.

Tony's mind was reeling. "That's madness! You want people to suffer so much that they surrender themselves to you? That's not control—that's enslavement!"

Jorthan shrugged. "Semantics. Call it what you will. In the end, humans will crawl to us, worshipping at our feet, not out of devotion, but out of fear." He turned to Dr. Upen. "And you have the final piece to complete it. The formula of the extract."

Jenny was confused. "When you have so much power and machines to control minds, you could have controlled Dr. Upen's mind and forced him to reveal, right?" she asked.

"Very good question, Miss…?" He looked at Jenny and then looked at Dr. Upen. "No wonder you pick talent for your team, Upen." He raised an eyebrow.

"Upen has never written it down dear. He knew this was not meant for anyone. He had also erased any trace of its existence until my boss 'Q' devised a means to put the scientists in a coma. His plan worked. Here we are!".

"Dr. Upen, Nyra and Jenny were shocked. So it was Jorthan and Q who were behind the plan all along.

"Do you think all this is a childish game?" Jorthan seemed angry, his nerves pulsing with reptilian responses. "No… This is one of the big plans from Q," he replied.

"What plans?" asked Jenny.
"Why do you think I will tell you?" laughed Jorthan.

Dr. Upen thought the only way to know was to trick him into revealing all his plans. "You'll never get the formula from me," he tried.

Jorthan laughed. "Upen, Upen.. You keep forgetting that my watch here—" he pointed to his watch, "…will alert me when you have genuinely decided to reveal the formula." he reminded.

Jorthan smirked. "But not just yet. We still have… unfinished business. You will reveal the formula soon, you have no choice…Q has given me power beyond imagination. I have so many powers now. I have even lost the count," he looked at his fingers.

"I have evolved beyond human limitations," he said with pride.

"Even after demonstrating my capabilities, my watch tells me that you are not ready to submit the formula."

"Hmm, you think you are strong, huh?" Jorthan contained his anger.

"Wait until you see my boss 'Q's powers." Jorthan pressed his lips.

He turned sharply to Mr. Chi. "I believe the time has come. Isn't that right, Q?"

A stunned silence filled the air. Tony, Lisha, Dr. Upen, Jenny, and Nyra froze, their eyes darting toward Mr. Chi.

Mr. Chi, still and emotionless, finally smiled—a slow, knowing smile. His skin flickered for a fraction of a second, almost imperceptibly. But it was enough.

Lisha noticed Mr. Chi standing unusually still. Unlike the others, he showed no reaction, no emotion. A strange unease settled in her mind.

Suddenly, the room's lighting changed, and started to flicker and finally, the lights went off.

The doors at the far ends of the lab closed with a deep hiss. The lights turned on and off.

A shadowy figure stepped forward, its form shifting slightly as it moved.

Dr. Upen's breath caught in his throat. Jenny and Nyra stared in shock. Tony fainted and fell on the floor.

Lisha's breath hitched. "No… it can't be…"

Without hesitation, Mr. Chi reached for the back of his head.
A faint click sounded, and a panel slid open, revealing a
grotesque fusion of reptilian nerves and mechanical circuits.

The truth hit them like a tidal wave.
Mr. Chi… was Q.

Mr. Chi—no, Q—tilted his head slightly like a reptile, his
voice smooth and calculated. "Oh, but it is." His voice
switching between human, reptile, robotic and alienist.

The room felt impossibly small. The air grew heavy with the
weight of realization.

Everything they thought they knew had been a lie.
The enemy had been with them all along.

❖

CHAPTER 5

NEVER EVER

"Protecting knowledge is greater than knowledge."

The atmosphere shifted as Q's expression turned grave. He stepped forward, his sharp gaze sweeping across the room.

"Boss, is it time to reveal the real reason why you have called them here?" Jorthan asked.

Q nodded and pressed a button. In an instant, the world leaders around the chamber flickered. Their eyes dimmed, and their movements jerked unnaturally. Then, with a single synchronized motion, they tilted their heads forward, exposing the intricate web of wires embedded into their skulls.

A ripple of horror passed through the room. The world leaders were not real humans. They were alien clones.

Jenny and Nyra gasped, their hands covering their mouths as the reality dawned on them.

Dr. Upen staggered backward, his mind unable to process the unimaginable horror unfolding before him.

How could he not have known? These leaders behaved exactly like humans—how? When? The questions swirled chaotically in his mind.

Was this a simulation? Had they ever been in control?

Jorthan was right. Q's reach was terrifying.

But Dr. Upen knew one thing for certain—Q's interest in the extract formula wasn't just about science. It was about something much bigger. But why?

Q let out a deep sigh, spinning his fidget between his fingers. His voice, distorted and unnatural, shifted between alien, reptilian, human, and robotic tones.

"Plans within plans."

He strode toward the massive supercomputer at the heart of the laboratory. With a deliberate motion, he inserted an encrypted pen drive, its surface etched with a cryptic insignia, into a specialized data port. Instantly, the system came to life.

The room dimmed as blue holographic grids materialized midair, forming a colossal projection across the entire wall.

Data streams cascaded at blinding speed, flashing across network nodes and high-frequency algorithms.

The sheer scale of information processing was beyond human comprehension.

Then, in bold red letters, the screen displayed:

HUMAN DATA COLLECTION - LIVE FEED

A heavy silence filled the room. Then, the projection zoomed out, revealing global maps, real-time movement tracking, biometric data streams, and intricate behavioral analytics of millions of people.

The screen displayed world leaders—both in the chamber and outside—alongside their real-time health metrics: heart rate, oxygen levels, and neural activity.

Lisha and Tony exchanged uneasy glances.

A deep, unsettling feeling clawed at Lisha's chest. She clenched her fists as the full weight of what she was seeing sank in.

This wasn't just data.

This was total surveillance.

ABSOLUTE CONTROL.

Dr. Upen felt a creeping realization take hold. This wasn't just about the expedition. This was the end of the world order— and it was now in alien hands.

"How did you even accomplish this?" Tony demanded.

A stunned silence followed.
Jorthan's voice broke the silence, calm and resolute. "We controlled everything through the world leaders, used global research funds for a secret, unauthorized project, and set up the network and channels of destruction."

"This is unacceptable—Yes, for humans but not for aliens," Jorthan added coldly.

"You had no right to experiment with human data like this!" Dr. Upen exclaimed.

Q remained unshaken. Instead, he let out a slow, knowing chuckle. Without a word, he reached into his pocket, pulling out a small metallic fidget spinner. His fingers played with it for a moment before pressing a hidden button on its surface.

A strange etheric halo pulsed outward. The room shimmered, a force sweeping over them. Before anyone could react, an invisible energy locked every person into their seats.

Gasps filled the air. No one could move—only their heads remained free.

Q took his time, his smirk deepening as he walked slowly around the room. Then, in a voice both calm and chilling, he began to reveal his greatest secret.

"You all want to know how I did it?" he mused. "Very well... Listen closely."

The projection behind him shifted, now displaying complex strands of code interwoven with DNA sequences.

A collective gasp filled the chamber.

Q continued, his eyes gleaming with an otherworldly glow. "Qrox is a planet far away from Earth, teeming with intelligent life. And if I control Earth, I will claim my rightful place as the ruler of Qrox itself."

His smirk deepened. "You see, I love control. I thrive on it."

"But my father... he disapproved of my methods. He saw me as flawed, unworthy to rule. He believed I was too consumed by my impulses. So, as punishment, he exiled me here, to this so called sacred Earth, to teach me a lesson."

He let out a hollow laugh. "But I couldn't resist. The need to dominate, to manipulate—it's in my nature."

Q paused, his smile turning darker. "So, I found a way around it. When I sneezed, I still carried the virus from my galaxy. I manipulated its strands, transforming it into a waterborne

contagion. One by one, we infected the world leaders—
Jorthan met each of them under the pretext of a project,
ensuring they consumed the tainted water. Each perished,
replaced seamlessly by my clones. The world was now under
my control."

He gestured toward the holographic display, where DNA
sequences flickered ominously.

"Then, I orchestrated a global pandemic. The so-called
vaccine? A mere facade. It scanned their DNA, feeding it
directly into my central database."

"Humans are so easy to manipulate," he laughed.

The screen behind him pulsed as a vast genetic archive
materialized in the air. "And finally, I wanted to play with
humans myself... so I cloned myself."

He gestured toward himself as if allowing everyone to scan
his body from head to toe.

The room remained frozen in horror as he leaned in closer,
his voice dropping to a whisper.

"I gave myself a new name..."

A sudden flicker in the holographic display caught their
attention. Q raised his hand, index and middle fingers

extended as if conducting an unseen force. The green-lit letters in the air reformed, shifting at his command.

C... H... I... A... M...

The letters pulsed, rearranged and glowed brighter.

Then, with a slow, deliberate movement, Q traced his fingers in the air, encircling the 'C' and twisting the 'H' in a way that seamlessly reshaped them into a single, complete form.

'C' transformed into a crescent circle.

'H' stretched, its arms curving, while one of the lines from 'H' coiled like a reptile, merging into the circular outline.

The chamber held its breath as the final symbol materialized.

'Q'

Now the display glowed...

Ch.. I.. AM.. and another flick of symbols.

Q.. I... AM...

and another flick of symbols.

I.. AM.. Q..

A shiver ran down their spines.

Q let his hand fall. The hologram flickered one last time before stabilizing.

"I am Q," he whispered, his voice a symphony of distorted frequencies.

Lisha's breath caught in her throat, while Tony watched helplessly. They had never been dealing with Mr. Chi. They had been dealing with Q all along.

Mr. Jorthan pitched as the holographic display flickered again. "You see, Q was always behind the mysterious events you struggled to understand," he said, his voice dripping with satisfaction.

Dr. Upen's eyes widened. "You mean… the disappearances? The strange anomalies? The inexplicable shifts in power?"

"Exactly," Jorthan interjected, stepping forward. "The president of Egypt—the one who pushed for Project Arizona's so-called treasure expedition—he wasn't human. He was one of Q's clones."

Nyra was shocked. They couldn't digest all this. "How could she not realize the clone all this while working with him?"

"It was never about treasure," Jorthan continued. "It was a ploy to lure you in, Upen. You were the most sought-after scientist, the only one with the knowledge we needed. But you outmaneuvered our plans, sending your interns Janani and Narmada instead."

Dr. Upen clenched his fists. "So it was you who put the brilliant scientists to a coma in the Arizona project treasure expedition…?"

Jorthan nodded. "Yes. We ensured those ten scientists consumed the Qrox-infected virus in their water bottles. Once they went into a coma, we eagerly waited for you to come forward and reveal the formula to save them. After all, you would do anything to hold your image — The science savior. Right?" He moved his brows.

"But despite our efforts, you still didn't reveal the formula."

Dr. Upen felt a wave of nausea. He had always suspected something was wrong with that expedition, but this… this was beyond anything he had imagined.

"But you had a plan," Q said, staring directly at Dr. Upen. "You handed over an extract that had been prepared long ago, not the actual formula. You tricked us."

Dr. Upen remained silent, his mind racing.
"That's why Mr. Chi called for Protocol-22," Lisha whispered. "To bring a device that could scan the extract's properties."
Lisha's instinct was correct.

"But why?" Dr. Upen's voice was sharp. "Why do you need more of it?"

Mr. Chi's gaze darkened. "Because one sample isn't enough. We need it for billions."

Dr. Upen felt a chill crawl down his spine. "Billions?"

Jorthan took a step forward. "And that's why you have no choice. You will reveal the formula, or humanity will perish."

A chilling silence gripped the room.

"Billions?" Dr. Upen's voice was barely above a whisper. "Why?"

Jorthan smirked. "Think, Upen! Think!"
"What is the ONE resource every human depends on daily?"

"Water."

Dr. Upen's breath hitched. "You… You mean—?"

Q's expression was eerily calm. "Yes. The Qrox virus will be mixed into every ocean, every sea, and every drinking source on this planet. People will consume it unknowingly, through the very essence of their survival. And one by one… they will fall into a coma."

Dr. Upen's body tensed as the horrifying realization dawned on him.

Q continued, his voice smooth, almost hypnotic.
"And when the world panics, the cloned leaders will sponsor a cure—a miracle solution to revive the fallen. Of course, that cure will come at a cost. Not in wealth. Not in power. But in submission. Humanity will beg for mercy, pleading for release from the suffering, from the torment, from the agony of half-life." He leaned closer, his alien eyes gleaming. "And in the end, they will beg… for death."

Dr. Upen felt his knees weaken. His mind spiraled into chaos.

Every fibre of his being screamed at him to fight, to resist, to break free—but how?

He squeezed his eyes shut. "I can't let this happen. Think… think!" he told himself. In that darkness, a voice echoed from the depths of his soul.

He recalled Babaji's words.
"This is one of nature's treasured secrets. It should never be written down. Never be shared with the wrong hands."

His breath became shallow. The weight of his life's work, the discoveries, the sacrifices, the countless lives he had saved—all of it flooded his mind in a tidal wave of emotion. Had it all come to this?

Tears slipped down his cheeks. He had always believed in using science for the good of humanity. But now, his greatest achievement—the formula—was the key to its enslavement.

A cruel choice stood before him. Reveal the formula, and condemn the earthlings to eternal torture. Or die, taking the secret with him.

Dr. Upen's hands clenched into fists. His chest heaved as he lifted his head, eyes burning with defiance.

With every ounce of strength left in him, he roared—

"N E V E R"
"NEVER WILL I EVER REVEAL THE FORMULA!"

The room fell still. Nyra and Jenny were terrified by that scream. They had never seen Dr. Upen in that aggression before. His voice thundered across the chamber, shaking the walls with its raw power.

"NEVER...."
"NEVER... EVER...."

Tears dripped but Dr. Upen did not budge. Slowly, angered and helpless at the same time, he dropped to his knees. He felt sad for the people of the world, a deep sorrow weighing down on him."

❖

CHAPTER 6

BOOM

"When arrogance peaks, fate speaks."

For a fleeting moment, silence reigned. Then the lights dimmed. The air grew colder. And Q... smiled. He was ready with his next move.

Beep. Beep.

"Initiating system... checksum OK... directories loaded..."

Holographic screens flickered and flashed symbols of human beings across the panels inside a secret laboratory.

Beep... Beep... Beep...
Three more sharp beeps filled the air, building up tension inside the high-tech chamber.

"Yes! Yes! The system is working!" shouted Jorthan, his excitement barely contained.

The connection had been established. "Finally, the day has arrived. I have waited many years for this day," said Jorthan, a sinister grin spreading across his face.

The flickering screens confirmed each step, displaying strange symbols and graphs that only a few could understand.

The entire chamber seemed to vibrate with energy, as if it were alive, buzzing with an electric force that hummed through the air.

"System loading…"

"Project Arizona starting…"

"Deployment in 10 minutes…"

The robotic voices echoed in unison. "Mission activated."

Tuck-tuck-tuck.

Footsteps echoed—measured, deliberate, controlled. The clones turned toward the sound, waiting. A slow, menacing laugh filled the chamber as a tall figure stepped forward from the shadows.

Mr. Chi was gone. Q had taken over. His human disguise had fully vanished. Now, in his true form, Q stood tall, his alien body radiating an eerie, otherworldly glow. His skin, a shifting mix of silver and deep blue, reflected the pulsing lights around him. His eyes, two burning golden orbs, flickered with intelligence and malice. A sharp ridge ran down the centre of his forehead, glowing faintly as if carrying an immense, hidden power.

Q approached the control panel at the centre of the chamber. With a press of a single button, the room transformed. The air thickened with invisible energy.

And then—
A towering holographic projection flickered to life.

A powerful being appeared, its presence commanding, its expression unreadable. This was not just any figure.

This was the King of Qrox. The father of Q.
A deep, ancient voice echoed through the chamber, filling every corner with a weight that pressed against the skin.

"Q, what is the reason for contacting me? Do you realize that using this connection will drain your soul power? Every time you reach out from Earth, you grow weaker."

Q's glowing eyes narrowed. "Father, I connected to remind you of your promise. You challenged me—if I take control of Earth, you will name me the next ruler of Qrox."

The king let out a heavy sigh. "Q, you waste your strength with your impatience. Tell me, have you succeeded?"

"Father, I am on the brink of total domination. One final move. I reached out to ensure that once Earth belongs to me, you will fulfill your word."

The king's expression remained unmoved. "You still have not changed, Q. Earth is not so easy to control. Its people are unpredictable. Their evolution has been a mystery forever. "

Q's jaw clenched. "You never appreciate my work! For many human years, I have cloned my kind into human forms. They can change shape using my genetic imprint, all controlled by the machine in this chamber. I have infiltrated every government on this planet. I have poisoned their food, their water, their very air—breaking their immune systems physically, mentally, and emotionally… everything… everything. Weakening them bit by bit, keeping them anxious, depressed, and ignorant."

The king's expression darkened. "Weakening their bodies does not mean you control them."

Q smirked. "That is where my greatest invention comes in. This new firmware will complete my mission. I will not only weaken their bodies—I will seize their minds." He paused.

"They will become my slaves, their wills erased. And once all of Earth bows to me, will you finally accept me as the rightful heir?" His voice became cold and sharp reflecting his strong determination.

The king's voice grew cold. "Again, I ask you—have you truly succeeded? Speak to me only after you succeed. Until then, you are nothing. And remember—as long as Siddha Targra remains, you can never control the world."

Q's expression twisted in fury. "Targra! Targra! Targra! You keep bringing up that name every single time! Targra cannot live with the humans anymore. I have already sent him where he belongs—to Zhautren's grave!"

At the mention of that name, the room fell into absolute silence.

Jenny, Nyra, Lisha, Tony, and Dr. Upen froze.

Zhautren.

The name sent a chill down their spines. Their eyes widened in disbelief.

This was impossible.

The world had dismissed Zhautren and her pursuits as a myth—a legend about an Egyptian princess who had disappeared into a pyramid during the last great galactic alignment.

Now, here they were. It all made sense. That was why to resurrect his sister Zhautren, Q and Jorthan devised the project Arizona Treasure Expedition.

Hearing from the mouth of Q's father himself—Zhautren was not a legend — She was real.

And worse—she was Q's sister.
Jenny's mind raced. "This… this can't be true! If Zhautren was real, then that means—"

Nyra's voice was barely a whisper. "Everything we knew about Project Arizona… was not just about treasure expeditions. It was indeed an extremely clever and dangerous plan by Q to resurrect Zhautren."

Nyra continued. "According to the myth, all these years, we thought she never returned because she perished inside the pyramid. But what if she never died? What if she's still alive?"

Jenny's voice shook. "And if she is, then where is she now?"

The king's holographic figure flickered, his eyes locking onto Q. "Your sister had the same foolish ambition as you. And just like you, she failed."

"Q, I give you one last warning—leave Earth and return to Qrox. You cannot win."

Q's lips curled into a twisted grin. "No, no, no, Father. You underestimate me. You always have. And soon, I will prove you wrong."

The king's image vanished. He was visibly disappointed by Q's arrogance.

Q turned to his clones, his voice sharp and unwavering. His anger burned within him, hotter than ever before.

He clenched his fists, his determination unshakable. He was not just fighting for himself—but also his sister to prove his father wrong. To prove that he was worthy of ruling over Earthlings.

This was it. The moment history would never forget — The final test of humanity's strength after so many years of evolution. Humans had dominated the land, plants and animals. Now it was an inter-planetary attack. Alien versus humans. Could humans survive the super intelligence and Q's attack?
The second galactic alignment was fast approaching, only weeks away. One by one, the planets of this solar system were falling into perfect alignment—an event of cosmic significance.

In the last galactic alignment something mysterious had happened when Zhautren was at the pyramid. A force beyond understanding had been unleashed.

And now… it was about to happen again.

What would this alignment bring? Would it mark Q's ultimate victory?

Or would it awaken something even more powerful?

Shaking announcements filled up the chamber.

"5…4…3…2…1…" — The moment was here.

"Deploy."

Then—
BOOM.
A surge of electromagnetic energy crashed against the Earth's outer atmosphere.

A shockwave rippled across the chamber, causing the lights to flicker and the very walls to tremble.

BOOM.
A second strike.
The air itself vibrated, as though reality was shifting under the force of something unseen.

BOOM.
The alien invasion had begun.

CHAPTER 7

CONFUSION OR CHAOS

"The greatest deception is believing we are in control."

Pacific Ocean | United Airlines Flight 839 | 10:23 PM

Eight-year-old Emily Carter pressed her nose against the cold airplane window, her eyes wide with wonder. The world below was a vast, endless blackness interrupted by the shimmering lights of distant cities. Her mother, Sarah, was fast asleep beside her, her head resting on the seat's cushion.

The plane was cruising steadily above the Pacific Ocean on its route from Los Angeles to Sydney when suddenly—

BOOM.

The entire aircraft trembled.

A strange force seemed to push against the plane's body. Emily gasped as she saw the stars outside shift as if the entire sky had moved.

The plane began veering to the right, then suddenly jerked back, as though it had been yanked in the opposite direction.

"Mom! Wake up!" Emily shook her mother frantically. "The plane—it reversed!"

Sarah groggily opened her eyes, frowning. "Honey, the plane's not supposed to go backward. What—?"

The captain's voice crackled through the speakers. "Ladies and gentlemen, this is your captain speaking. We are experiencing an unexplained shift in our navigation system. I assure you there is no immediate cause for concern."

Emily's small fingers clutched the armrest. The passengers were murmuring, some looking at their watches. "It was clear the direction had changed—but why?"

Down below, at Honolulu International Airport, air traffic controllers were in disarray. Multiple flights were reporting course deviations, yet instruments showed nothing wrong. Something unnatural was altering their paths.

Indian Ocean | RAAF VIP Aircraft | 5:45 AM

Onboard the Royal Australian Air Force VIP Aircraft, Minister Hugh Pearce was in discussion with his chief advisors. They were halfway through their diplomatic journey when an alert flashed on the flight panel.

"Sir, we have deviated from our planned course," said the pilot over the intercom.

The minister frowned. "What do you mean deviated? We're flying on autopilot."

The chief security officer stood up, his face pale. "Sir… we're not flying towards India anymore. We're turning southeast… towards Antarctica."

A tense silence filled the cabin.

"Antarctica? That's impossible! How?" Walters demanded. Meanwhile, in the Canberra Air Traffic Control Center, operators were scrambling to make sense of the event.

All communication with the minister's aircraft had gone silent. The signal was active, but there was no response.

"Something's hijacking our navigation," muttered a controller.

Maldives | Beachfront Resort | 6:15 AM

Tourists enjoyed an early morning parasailing session over the calm Indian Ocean when the winds suddenly shifted.

"Hey! The parachute's moving sideways!" yelled one of the instructors.

A couple filming with a drone noticed something strange—
the sea waves were oscillating in erratic patterns.

The drone's compass showed incorrect readings.

One of the instructors radioed in. "Control, we're seeing some
unnatural wave behavior. Also, our guests in the sky are
drifting further out even though the wind hadn't changed.
What's happening?"

On the shores, Malé International Airport was receiving flight
distress signals—every plane in the sky was off course.

Bhutan | Remote Village | 8:10 AM UTC+6

In a small village nestled in the mountains, Dawa, a young
boy, clutched his pet cat as he watched a strange sight—
hundreds of rats, snakes and insects were scurrying out of
the ground.

"Grandmother, look! The animals are acting strange!"

His grandmother stepped out of their hut and gasped.
Birds were circling wildly in the sky.

The cattle were restless, their eyes darting around as if
sensing an unseen predator.

Something was wrong with the earth itself.

Nepal | Pashupatinath Temple | 8:45 AM

At one of Nepal's holiest temples, monks paused their morning prayers. Pigeons that roosted in the temple's rafters erupted into the air in a frenzied panic.

Then, a deep rumbling began beneath their feet.

The temple bells swung without being touched. The sacred water from the Bagmati River receded unnaturally, revealing its dry riverbed for a brief moment before flooding back.

Birds were circling wildly. Pilgrims gasped in terror.

Kenya | Nairobi National Park | 9:30 AM

Dr. Elijah Kalu, a senior zookeeper, stared in horror at the lions' enclosure.

The normally proud and composed predators were cowering, their tails tucked between their legs.

"Something is terrifying them… but what?" he muttered.

The elephants trumpeted loudly, pacing nervously. The giraffes huddled in a defensive cluster. Even the usually aggressive hyenas whimpered.

In the nearby Kenyan Meteorological Department, scientists recorded a bizarre shift in the Earth's magnetic field.

South Atlantic Ocean | Research Vessel "Aquamarine" | 12:15 PM

Marine biologists aboard Aquamarine were stunned.

"The fish are rising to the surface! This is highly unusual!" exclaimed Dr. Greg Mendes.

Sonar readings were erratic—deep-sea creatures that normally never surfaced were appearing near the waterline.

Then: an underwater tremor shook the vessel.

"What the—? That's not normal seismic activity!" one of the geologists cried.

The captain radioed into the Argentinian Oceanic Institute.

"We need answers. Now."

Washington, D.C. | Pentagon Situation Room | 3:30 PM

Inside the Pentagon, military officials gathered, staring at global reports.

Something unprecedented was happening.

"We have lost contact with several VIP flights. Animals worldwide are behaving abnormally. Weather patterns are fluctuating despite clear forecasts. Our satellites..." the communications officer hesitated, "...are picking up an unknown interference."

The Secretary of Defense turned to the room. "Where is the President? We need his orders."

The room fell silent.

The White House staff exchanged uneasy glances. Then, finally, the Chief of Staff spoke.

"Sir... The President is missing."

Gasps filled the room.

"Missing? What do you mean missing?!" demanded an official.

"He's gone—vanished without a trace. And it's not just him. We've received reports that world leaders across the globe are... unaccounted for."

A chill spread through the room.

This wasn't a natural disaster.

It was something else.

Something terrifying.

And no one was in charge anymore.

The world was in chaos.

And no one knew what was coming next.

"EMERGENCY — Press the damn button— NOW!" The secretary ordered.

The "EMERGENCY" button was pressed that connected to the most secret and central server somewhere in the Arctic.

Global Crisis Communication | Classified Emergency Channels | 04:45 UTC

A red alert flashed across classified communication networks worldwide.

Government officials scrambled to assess the unprecedented aviation and technological anomalies, but an even more urgent crisis was unfolding—world leaders were missing.

Inside a high-security command centre in the Arctic, the World Defense Security Advisor, General Howard Briggs, stood with his arms crossed, eyes fixed on a map covered in blinking red indicators.

"We're officially in the dark, people. Radar reports make no sense. We have planes shifting trajectory without pilot control, satellites flickering out of existence for seconds at a time, and now, the most alarming development yet—The President is gone."

A hush fell over the room. His words carried a weight that sent chills down spines.

"Gone?" A senior officer echoed.

Briggs's jaw tightened. "Vanished. Off the grid. No official logs of travel. No emergency protocols triggered. Just... gone."

An emergency line buzzed on the console. The United Kingdom was calling.

London, UK | Prime Minister's Emergency Office

"This is Deputy PM, Catherine Wallace. We have an urgent situation. The Prime Minister's whereabouts are unknown. We have no logs of official travel, and his security team has gone silent."

Briggs exchanged glances with his intelligence officer. "Same here in the U.S. We can't reach our President either."

A third line blinked—France was calling.

Paris, France | Élysée Palace

The French Minister of Defense spoke rapidly. "You're telling me your leaders are missing too? Our President left for an undisclosed 'diplomatic mission' two days ago. He was scheduled to check in—radio silence. What on earth is going on?"

A fourth line lit up. India.

New Delhi, India | National Security Headquarters

The Indian Foreign Secretary, voice tense, cut straight to the point. "We have a crisis on our hands. Our Prime Minister left for an off-the-record meeting. He has not returned, and we cannot establish contact."

The realization hit them all like a crashing wave.

Washington, London, Paris, New Delhi—every country leader had disappeared.

Beijing, China | People's Liberation Army Command Center

A stern-looking Chinese Military Strategist spoke next. "We assumed the U.S. was behind this. But if your leader is missing too, then this is something bigger."

Moscow, Russia | Kremlin War Room

A senior Russian General chimed in, his voice gruff and suspicious. "We don't like coincidences. This isn't a simple disappearance. This is a calculated maneuver."

The discussion escalated. Speculation turned into fear.

"Could it be a hijacking? Some kind of synchronized abduction?"

"Or worse… a global military coup?"

"A cyber attack? Something that has overridden our tracking systems?"
"A nuclear strike preparation? If this is an act of war, we are completely unprepared."

More calls flooded in—Germany, Australia, Japan, South Africa, and Brazil. Each with the same chilling update.

All their leaders had vanished. A weighted silence fell over the global communication channels. It was unthinkable.

Then someone voiced the terrifying thought on everyone's mind: "If they're all gone… who is controlling the world?"

CHAPTER 8

BREAKING NEWS

"Perception is more powerful than reality."

"Breaking News! Breaking News!" shouted Bhaskar, the editor of a popular TV news channel, barging into the meeting room.

His voice boomed through the walls as he slammed a thick file onto the table, sending coffee cups rattling.

"Sir, next time, please speak softly. You're hurting my ears!" Pallavi winced, massaging her temple.

Bhaskar's sudden entry always felt like a mini heart attack. She silently cursed her boss for his complete disregard for people's eardrums.

Bhaskar, in his fifties with a belly that proudly announced his love for snacking, was never a serious editor. He treated his newsroom like a cricket match—full of excitement, last-minute sprints, and unnecessary shouting.

Ignoring Pallavi, he grinned. "Everyone's minds will explode when you see what's in these files!" He kept tapping the folder dramatically.

Pallavi rolled her eyes and smirked at her colleague. "Breaking news applies to him, not to us," she muttered. But as Bhaskar turned toward her, she quickly plastered on a fake smile.

"Well, where is our Miss Viral? I don't see her in this meeting. Somebody, please call her!" Bhaskar demanded, scanning the room.

"Sir, how can I call her? You banned phones in the office today," his secretary reminded him.

"Oh, yes, I did. Everything happens for a reason!" Bhaskar declared, striking a pose as if he had just delivered the ultimate wisdom.

The entire team groaned in unison.

"No, not again!" Pallavi muttered under her breath.

"He and his dialogues! How many times will he repeat them?" Akshara whispered.

"His wife must have nerves of steel," Pallavi smirked.

"She's deaf," Akshara said matter-of-factly. Pallavi gasped. "Oh my God, I've worked here for ten years and never knew that!"

"That," Akshara chuckled, "is breaking news!"

Before their giggles could continue, the door swung open.

"She is here, sir," announced KP, the team manager, as Aruzhla walked in.

"Come in, Miss Viral... I mean, sorry, Miss Aruzhla. Please take your seat," Bhaskar said, correcting himself, then dramatically announced, "Breaking News!"

Aruzhla was used to Bhaskar's antics. The name 'Miss Viral' had stuck to her after she had once mistakenly said on live TV, "This virus is going viral..." instead of "This virus is going global..." during a COVID report. The clip had gone viral, making her an internet sensation overnight.

Bhaskar clapped his hands together. "Alright, team! Get ready for a nationwide lockdown!"

Silence.
Then, chaos.

"What?" the team exclaimed in unison.

"I want this telecasted in the next 3 hours. This is the reason I banned phones today. Once this news is out, you'll all get flooded with calls—avoid them. No questions, no answers, and no political interference. Today, our TRP should explode!" Bhaskar grinned, making an upward rocket gesture.

"Sir, why don't you tell us first?" demanded Aruzhla. "Yeah!" the team chimed in.

Bhaskar leaned back, smiling. "Alright, alright, I can never say a 'No' to my Miss Virus—I mean, Miss Viral."
Aruzhla crossed her arms. "Sir, please, it's hard for me to know when you are serious and when you are not."

She continued, "First, you banned phones. Then we come to work and find the internet is down. What's happening?"

Bhaskar sighed and gestured toward the giant screen in the meeting room. "Well, take a look for yourselves."

The screen flickered to life. A video montage played from his USB drive, compiling viral clips from social media—X, Instagram, YouTube, TikTok. The team watched in stunned silence.

The Video Feed —

— Children sat in circles on playgrounds, whispering amongst themselves.

One kid leaned in, eyes wide. "Hey, did you see that? The swing just moved in circles… but no one was on it!"

Another kid smirked. "Pfft, that was me. You guys never believe me—I have superpowers like superheroes!"

The other kids looked at him with suspicion.
One raised an eyebrow. "Oh really? Move that see-saw right now, Super-kid."

The "superhero" hesitated. "Uh… I don't feel like it right now."

The others burst into laughter. "Yeah, right!"
Meanwhile, in the corner, a quiet girl whispered, "But… what if he's telling the truth?"

"No, He is just lying," said one of the kid. "I have watched many super hero movies".

"Ohhh - It must be the real avengers. They must be on a secret mission!" another declared. "They don't harm children, so nothing to worry. Come on guys, let's resume playing" he shouted.

— Doctors in operating rooms whispered between surgeries.

A surgeon adjusted his gloves. "I was in the OT, and the lights started flickering on and off. That was strange."

A nurse frowned. "That's nothing! The patient who never talks pointed at something floating above his bed. I swear, his eyes were wide like he'd seen a ghost!"

The anesthetist raised a hand. "Hold on. What if—now hear me out—this is a side effect of anesthesia? Like, they're seeing another dimension?"

The room fell silent.
Then, the intern chuckled. "Great. Another reason to avoid surgery."

The head surgeon sighed. "Enough! If ghosts want free surgeries, they better get in line!"

— Road workers leaned on their shovels, watching videos on their phones.

"I tell you, brother, this is how politicians start! First, they create false narratives and stories to trick people. Then BOOM—world war!"

"They'll say it's just a minor issue, nothing to worry about. Next thing you know, the markets crash, and everyone's blaming each other."

"Then suddenly, some big speech about national security, troops get deployed, and it's all over the news like nobody saw it coming."

"And we? We'll still be here, fixing these same damn roads, watching history repeat itself."

— Plumbers and electricians huddled over screens in repair shops.

"Maybe it's a military experiment gone wrong?"
"What if they're in another dimension?"

"Dude… you watch too much Netflix."

"What if it's some kind of glitch in the system?"
"Or maybe a massive power surge short-circuited reality itself."

— A scientist in a laboratory was on a live stream.

"Radars show no unusual movement. If it were a hijacking, we'd know. If it were a nuclear strike, we'd be dead. Then WHAT IS HAPPENING?"

The video ended.

Silence.

The newsroom team turned to Bhaskar.

Pallavi sipped her coffee. "So, what you're saying is… the world is officially losing its mind?"

Akshara shrugged. "We already know that. Let's announce something new."

KP, the manager, leaned back in his chair. "Sir, do we cover this as a crisis or a comedy special?"

Bhaskar slammed his hand on the table. "IDIOTS! This is history in the making!"

Aruzhla rubbed her temples. "Sir… where did the local politicians and the elected national leaders go?"

Bhaskar smirked. "Ah. That, my dear Miss Viral, is the million-dollar question."

The room fell silent once more.

Somewhere outside, the world panicked. But inside the newsroom, the game had just begun.

The expressions in the room were a mix of amusement and disbelief. Some looking at their coffee cups, some biting their lips, while some just raising their eyebrows pondering.

Rajan, the most skeptical of the bunch, crossed his arms. "Sir, I have a question."

Bhaskar leaned back in his chair, grinning. "Only one? Come on, Rajan. Ask ten! I love questions."

Rajan rolled his eyes. "Umm.." He cleared his throat —"How did you manage to get these different video footage? This isn't regular news channel content. Some of these look like very personal talks in their private places!"

The team murmured in agreement.

Bhaskar puffed his chest, dramatically adjusting his tie. "Ah, Rajan, my boy... You still don't know your boss, do you?" He leaned forward, lowering his voice as though revealing a state secret. "I have eyes everywhere. My network is stronger and faster than the Wi-Fi speeds you all keep complaining about."

Yogina in disbelief - "Oh really? Who are these mysterious people feeding you intel?"

Bhaskar grinned wider. "People who like money. You see when you pay well, people suddenly develop very sharp observational skills. Traffic cops, airport staff, train station workers, waiters at fancy hotels... Even those tea vendors outside government offices. They all work for me in some way. I invest in human surveillance."

The team exchanged looks, half-impressed, half-worried.

Pallavi shook her head. "I knew it. Bhaskar Sir is running his own secret intelligence agency. No wonder his wife keeps saying she doesn't know where he is half the time."

The room burst into laughter.

Bhaskar, loving the attention, dramatically raised a finger. "And that, my friends, is why I do everything for our news channel to gain more popularity. While other reporters are chasing political drama, I get you the real, raw footage."

Rajan, still skeptical, narrowed his eyes. "Sir, but… these are personal and private conversations happening in their spaces. Doctors whispering in operating rooms, kids chatting in playgrounds, even traffic cops discussing faulty signals—this isn't meant for public broadcast. Isn't it unethical to relay this without their consent?"

Bhaskar smirked, leaning forward. "Ah, Rajan… You're new here." He chuckled, shaking his head. "You really think I break the privacy rules? Oh no, my dear boy. I have a much better strategy."

Rajan looked confused. "What do you mean?"

Bhaskar clapped his hands together and grinned. "Simple. I make my own news. You see, I don't just rely on raw footage. I take inspiration from real incidents, gather details from my secret sources, and then… I have my drama team act it out."

Rajan's jaw dropped. "Wait… you mean this real raw footage you showed us now, is all going to be staged by your team of actors and put on screen?!"

Bhaskar nodded proudly. "A hundred per cent. And not just any actors—the best in the business. My people are trained to re-enact real-life situations with such precision that the audience thinks they're watching raw footage. And that's how our news goes viral, my boy!"

Rajan turned to the rest of the team, expecting them to be just as shocked. But instead, they all looked… completely unfazed. Some even smirked, waiting for his reaction.

Pallavi sighed, patting Rajan's shoulder. "Welcome to the real world, rookie. Bhaskar sir's way of doing news isn't about reporting what happened—it's about making sure people care about what's happening."

Akshara chuckled. "Yeah, and in times of uncertainty, nobody pays attention to plain facts. Drama sells, Rajan. And Bhaskar sir? He's a master of it."

Bhaskar took a dramatic bow. "Thank you, thank you! At least someone appreciates my genius."

Rajan still looked horrified. "But… isn't this misleading? This is literally manufacturing news!"

Bhaskar waved his hand dismissively. "Oh, please. It's not fake news, Rajan. It's just… enhanced reality. I'm only helping people visualize things better."

Rajan buried his face in his hands. "I can't believe this. I joined a drama company, not a news channel."

Rajan continued, his voice filled with doubt, "If you're saying we should start telecasting news in the next 3 hours... how can you get your actors to recreate these video scenes so quickly? What about the backgrounds, the artifacts, and the entire setup? How will you find the time for all that?"

The team burst into laughter, clearly enjoying his bewilderment.

Dennis, grinning, leaned forward. "Just behind the washroom, there's a small passage that says 'Staff Only'... and behind it is the entire theatre setup, Rajan. It's like a movie set but for news. Hospitals, theaters, schools, roads, seas, skies—you name it. Everything is there. The projector scans video footage and instantly recreates the scene behind. And the whole setup is ready in minutes."

He paused, watching Rajan's face as the realization started to sink in. "If Bhaskar's already this prepared for everything, I'm sure he's got it all covered. The actors are probably already in costume, eating snacks, waiting for their cue. Right boss?" Dennis chuckled, clearly amused by Rajan's confusion.

Rajan, still processing, began to wave his fingers in the air as though mentally trying to organize all the directions and possibilities. His mind was racing, and the idea of instantaneous scene creation felt like something amazing.

Unvi, noticing his deep thought, couldn't resist the opportunity for a little jab. "Are you planning to change your job from a news team assistant to acting? Rajan?" she asked with a smirk, the entire team bursting into laughter once again.

Rajan blinked, slightly taken aback, as he finally realized how far out of his depth he was. "Great. So basically, we work for a news mafia." he sighed.

Bhaskar beamed. "Exactly! And proud of it! Now, let's get this on air before anyone else does!"

Bhaskar slapped Rajan's back who was seemingly lost. "Relax, my boy. Now, let's get this on air! We have an entire country to entertain," he reiterated.

"Breaking news! Breaking news... Come on, that's what I want to keep hearing from now on." He said, waiting for his team to join him.

The team was still processing the gravity of the situation, their minds racing to piece together the fragments of what they had just been briefed on. Deep down, they all suspected it was just some glitch being blown out of proportion by

Bhaskar. But none of them dared to speak up; after all, he paid them handsomely, and they weren't about to jeopardize that. All except Aruzhla. Though she pretended to be unfazed, something felt different this time. Deep within, she sensed they were on the brink of something monumental—something bigger than anything they had encountered before.

CHAPTER 9

MYSTERIOUS BREEZE

"Nature is your untouched wisdom in its purest form."

The "no phones" rule had worked wonders. Bhaskar had insisted that all the team members, both on and off-air, had to adhere to this rule during the broadcast of his news channel.

There were no interruptions, no distractions, no time wasted scrolling through social media or answering unnecessary calls. The result was nothing short of extraordinary.

The news channel continued to broadcast one sensational show after another, with viewership skyrocketing. The TRP ratings surged like a tidal wave, shattering all previous records — with no other show in the country coming close.

As the hours ticked by, the team noticed that they were becoming part of something bigger than they had anticipated.

The air in the newsroom was electric, the kind of atmosphere that can only be created when something truly groundbreaking is happening.

The production staff worked tirelessly behind the scenes, the anchors delivered the news in their perfected dramatic style, and even the technical team worked in perfect synchrony, making sure every broadcast went off without a hitch.

Bhaskar couldn't contain his joy. His face beamed with pride every time the TRP graph shot upward. He smiled as if he were witnessing a rocket launch with each rising number.

It was a victory for him, for his vision, and for the entire team who had bought into his philosophy. No questions asked, no answers expected. It was just his way and right now, it seemed like everything was falling into place.

By the end of the night, Bhaskar's channel had topped the number one spot again. The team watched in awe as the TRP chart continued to climb, the numbers reflecting their hard work and Bhaskar's relentless pursuit of success.

As the evening wore on and the last show concluded, Bhaskar turned to Aruzhla, who had been the backbone of the team's success.

"Excuse me, sir?" voiced Aruzhla.

"Yes! Yes.. my sweet Miss Viralah," Bhaskar said, calling her with a sense of admiration, "I mean, Miss... Miss... Aruzhla." he stammered, correcting himself. He tried to rhyme her name with an affectionate twist.

His words spilled out playfully, but the sincerity in his tone was evident. "I can never say a 'no' to you. You're the reason our channel is gaining popularity. All thanks to your brilliant coverage, your cute smile, and, of course, your hard work." Aruzhla, who had been keeping her head down as she looked at final reports, felt a mixture of pride and discomfort. Bhaskar's praise, though generous, always made her uneasy.

She didn't thrive on attention or accolades, but it was undeniable that her contributions were a significant part of their success. Yet, something was bothering her—something deeper than the usual tiredness she felt after long hours of work.

"Excuse me, sir," Aruzhla said quietly again, pinching her lips and raising her brows, almost as if asking for permission. She wasn't used to speaking up like this, and her voice was laced with hesitation.

Bhaskar turned to her immediately, his face lighting up with genuine affection. "What is it, Miss Virahla? You've got that look on your face like you're holding something back." He leaned forward in his chair, his eyes focused on her with intensity.

Aruzhla shifted uncomfortably in her seat, glancing down at the desk before speaking. "I... I'm not feeling too well, actually. I have a severe headache, and I just don't feel like myself today," she said softly, though her words were laced with hesitation. She wasn't one to complain, but the truth was, the constant pressure, long hours, and the emotional toll of working under Bhaskar's demanding leadership had begun to take its toll on her.

Bhaskar's face softened with concern. He had always prided himself on being attentive to his staff's well-being—at least when it suited his agenda.

"A headache?" he repeated, his voice full of affection, though the gears in his mind were already turning. "That's not good, not good at all. You need to rest. You've been working so hard today; you deserve a break."

"How about you take a break at the office rest areas? I have arranged for many spacious private rooms just behind our office. You can opt for whichever you prefer!" He hinted casually.

"Once you are better, you can just join us back, easy!" He smiled.

But Aruzhla, though tempted, wasn't one to accept a break so easily. She had a sense of duty that drove her to push through any discomfort.

"I was hoping... maybe I could leave for the night?" she asked, trying to mask her true feelings with a gentle request.

"I can rest at home and return tomorrow feeling better. And I don't want to accept the overtime pay either. I'll just head home."

"You know how things are now—things can change in an instant, and I need you to be ready to jump back in whenever necessary."

Aruzhla blinked, her mind racing. She had hoped for a brief reprieve, a moment to let her guard down, but Bhaskar wasn't one to grant such luxuries. It wasn't about her well-being; it was about keeping the machine running — keeping the news and the TRP continuously churning.

"But sir... I'm really not feeling well," she said quietly, trying to express her discomfort. "I think I really need to go home, sir. I can't focus properly if I stay here, and I'm sure I'll be much better if I rest tonight."

Bhaskar looked at her, his expression softening again, but this time, there was a hint of concern. He knew she wasn't one to ask for time off unless it was serious. You can work from home, but I need you to be ready to jump back in as soon as you're feeling better. Got it?"

Bhaskar's face twisted in mild surprise, but his smile remained as he leaned back in his chair. "Alright, alright," he said with a sigh. "But listen—since you're such an important part of this team, I need you to stay online and available."

"Conditions apply. You can work from home, of course, but I still need you online. You can take a break, but only from the office, not from the work itself. Your presence on the office chat is essential, and I need to make sure you're available."

"Please carry this special office phone. And keep this with you at all times." He said handing her the premium iFone model that had the latest AI and GPS navigation with satellite connectivity enabled for emergency communication.

Aruzhla could feel the weight of his words. Bhaskar's tone wasn't harsh, but the underlying command was unmistakable. She knew what he was implying—he was in control. She had no choice but to comply. She nodded, relief washing over her. "Sure, sir. I'll stay online."

"And don't worry," Bhaskar whispered almost as an afterthought, leaning in slightly. "You'll still get your overtime pay, even if you're at home. I know how important that is for you." He gave her a reassuring smile, his tone light but with that familiar, subtle manipulation she had grown accustomed to.

Aruzhla managed a small smile, grateful for his trick to keep her happy, but it didn't fool her. She knew Bhaskar all too well by now. He'd never let her fully rest, always keeping a watchful eye on his employees. "Thank you, sir," she said, though she was now eager to escape the intensity of the office for a moment.

Bhaskar looked at her, his smile wide and reassuring. "Of course, Miss Viralah, I know you'll come through for us. But remember, no excuses the day after tomorrow. We'll need you sharp and ready."

As Aruzhla gathered her things, she walked toward the exit. The hum of the newsroom was still alive behind her, but it felt a bit suffocating now. She made her way through the sea of desks, past the staff who were too focused on their work to notice her leaving, until one of her colleagues, Rhea, called out.

"Leaving already?" Rhea raised an eyebrow, clearly surprised. "Isn't it a little early for you to be heading out? What, are you too tired to finish the day? Some of us are still here pushing through the overtime."

Aruzhla smiled faintly, though her tiredness was evident. "Yeah, I'm not feeling too great. Headache, you know?" She waved her hand dismissively, but Rhea wasn't convinced.

Rhea leaned back in her chair, crossing her arms and giving Aruzhla a knowing look.

"Sure, a headache... I've heard that one before," she said with a smirk. "Must be nice, though, huh? Get to leave early, and still get paid for it."

Aruzhla's smile faltered slightly as she glanced at the rest of the team. They were all hunched over their desks, immersed in their work, and no one else seemed to have a problem with it. But Rhea's comment stung a little.

She knew that her colleagues often speculated about her relationship with Bhaskar, and the rumors had begun to spread over time. It wasn't easy being his most trusted employee, especially when people assumed she was getting special treatment.

"Yeah, I'm sure it's nice," Aruzhla replied, trying to keep her tone light. "But I'll be back online later. Don't worry, I'm not abandoning ship."

Rhea let out a short laugh. "Just don't take too long, or else we might start wondering if you're just getting a day off. Wouldn't want to miss the big pay either, right?"

Aruzhla forced a smile but felt the sting of Rhea's words. "I'll be back. No need to worry," she said, before quickly heading for the door.

As she exited the office, she could feel the weight of the long day settling in. She had to get away for a little while, even if it meant working from home. As soon as she stepped outside and breathed in the cool evening air, she felt a small sense of relief. The pressure of Bhaskar's expectations, the noise of the newsroom, and the constant push for success had become too much to bear.

The rest of the team remained behind, their work never truly done. As Bhaskar's empire continued to grow, the boundaries between personal life and work life began to blur. The team, fueled by the allure of money and success, kept grinding away. They were part of Bhaskar's vision, and no matter how demanding or exhausting it became, they would keep going. After all, this was the price of success.

The night sky was quiet, with the soft moonlight shining down on the streets. Aruzhla walked home, her heels clicking against the pavement. The city was still awake, but the sounds around her felt distant as if she was walking through a dream.

As she walked, a cool breeze suddenly blew, making her long hair flap over her eyes. It felt as if the wind was trying to tell her, "Look!"

But Aruzhla didn't pay much attention. She kept her head down, lost in her thoughts, and continued walking.

Just then, another gust of wind blew past her, carrying dust around her straight to her face. She kept ignoring it and continued walking.

When she reached the small temple at the corner of the street, another strong breeze swept past her. This time, it carried dry banyan leaves from the ground, sending them flying into the air. One leaf, larger than the rest, spun in circles before landing right on her cheek.

Aruzhla gently peeled it off her skin and looked at it for a moment.

But something strange caught her attention. This leaf was different. It wasn't just any ordinary dry leaf. It had golden-brown veins running through it, making it look like tiny rivers flowing across its surface. The edges curled slightly, giving it an old, wise appearance. Strangely, despite being dry, the leaf was soft to touch—almost like silk.

She knew banyan leaves were special, and she didn't want them to be trampled on by people walking by.

"But there are so many banyan leaves scattered here. I can't clean all of them." she thought. "Anyways, it's just this one special leaf that fell on me, so at least this leaf I can make sure nobody steps on it." she thought looking around for a safe place.

"Ah! This is a good spot to place the leaf!" She said to herself, looking at a small idol nearby.

She stepped closer to the temple, where there was a statue of a snake god under a big banyan tree. Carefully, Aruzhla placed the special leaf near the idol, making sure it wouldn't be blown away again.

A sadhu (a holy man) wearing a turban with large peacock feathers was sitting nearby. He had been sitting still, lost in deep thought. But when Aruzhla placed the leaf down, he slowly turned his head and looked at her. His eyes were calm, and he seemed to notice her kind act.

The temple doors were being closed. Standing in front of the temple, Aruzhla touched her chin with her fingers and closed her eyes for a moment. She whispered a silent prayer in her heart before continuing on her way.

Just as she opened her eyes, something made her glance up. Her gaze met the sadhu's. He was still watching her, his deep-set eyes locked onto hers. A shiver ran down her spine. There was something strange about the way he looked at her—not unkind, but knowing as if he understood something she didn't.

The moment their eyes met, the sadhu quickly turned away, as if he didn't want to be caught staring. Aruzhla's heartbeat quickened. For a second, she felt uneasy.

The wind picked up again, rustling the branches of the banyan tree. The leaves whispered against each other, almost like voices speaking in hushed tones.

A cool shiver ran down her spine. She wasn't sure why she felt uneasy, but she pushed the feeling aside.

"It's just a temple, just an old man", she told herself. She took a deep breath and walked away.

As she left, the wind swirled around the temple once more, lifting the dry leaves into the air. The banyan branches rustled as if whispering a secret—one that Aruzhla was not ready to hear.
Without looking back, she continued her walk home.

But behind her, the sadhu remained still, his gaze now following her retreating figure. The wind swirled around the temple once more, as if it had tried—and failed—to deliver a message.

From a distance, Aruzhla saw that she was closer to her house. "Finally!" She forced her sleepy eyes. She fumbled for her keys in the depths of her purse, the jangle of metal against metal a comforting sound amidst the chaos of her confused thoughts.

By the time Aruzhla reached home, she felt exhausted. As the door swung open, she was greeted by the warm embrace of her mother, her smile radiant despite the lines of worry etched upon her face.

"Welcome home, darling," she said, her voice soft with concern. "How was your day?"

Aruzhla returned her mother's embrace, the familiar scent of home enveloping her in a sense of security she had longed for.

"It was... eventful," she admitted with a weary smile, her eyes betraying the exhaustion that clung to her like a shadow.

Just then, her younger brother, ten-year-old Jittu, ran into the room, waving the TV remote. "Aru! Guess what? I finished Shaktimaan episode 100! It was awesome!"

Her younger brother was a bundle of energy and mischief. His voice was always filled with the exuberance of youth.

"You should see the repeat telecast tomorrow!" He demanded slightly teasing her with a welcoming bum dance.

Aruzhla laughed. "I'll take your word for it, little bro," she said, ruffling his hair. Her heart swelled with affection for the spirited young boy who never failed to brighten her darkest days.

She made her way further into the cozy confines of their home. "Mom, could you please set dinner on the table? I'm craving your food." Aruzhla requested with a hint of urgency in her voice, her stomach growling in protest. As she sat down to eat, her mind drifted away to events she recounted happened that day.

With a loving smile, Aruzhla's mother smoothed a stray strand of hair behind her daughter's ear and straightened her dress, her touch conveying a silent reassurance. "Come, dear, sit and eat," she encouraged, pulling out a chair at the table.

Aruzhla picked up her fork, and her gaze drifted into the distance, lost in a sea of thought.

Dinner was warm and comforting. As she ate, her thoughts drifted back to the temple, the strange leaf, and the sadhu's deep gaze. A part of her wanted to forget it, but another part of her felt something was left unfinished.

But even as she settled into the familiar comfort of her surroundings, a nagging sense of unease gnawed at the edges of her consciousness, a feeling that something was amiss, something important that she couldn't quite put her finger on. It wasn't her mood, something else. Was it intuition?

After dinner, she stood up. "Good night, Mom! Good night, Jittu!"

"Gudnite" Jittu screamed from the sofa.

"Sleep well, my dear," her mother said, gently brushing her hair back.

She quickly finished her night routine, applied skin moisturizer and quickly wore her night pajamas.

In her bedroom, the air felt heavy. Aruzhla pushed the curtains aside and opened the window. A cool gust of wind rushed in, brushing against her face. She sighed, letting the fresh air soothe her tired body.

Without a second thought, she collapsed onto her bed. The moment her head touched the pillow, sleep took over. She was too exhausted to notice that the window was still open, its frame rattling slightly in the wind.

Then, the strange winds returned. A mysterious air continued to blow from her window.

The curtains swayed, lifting and twisting as if invisible hands were playing with them. A soft humming sound filled the room, a whisper in the air—gentle, yet carrying something unknown.

For in the heart of the modern world, amidst the hustle and bustle of everyday life, a missing leaf fluttered in the wind, its secrets waiting to be uncovered by those brave enough to seek the truth.

And then it happened.

The special leaf, carried by the wind, drifted in through the open window. It twirled in slow circles, floating weightlessly as if it had a mind of its own. It was the same special leaf—the one she had picked up from the temple grounds, the one she had placed near the snake idol.

The golden-brown veins glowed faintly in the dim moonlight. Its curled edges trembled as the wind guided it forward. It cycled through the air before falling gently onto Aruzhla's face.

For a moment, the leaf rested there, as if waiting for her to wake up.

But she didn't.

She was deep in sleep, unaware of nature's mysterious ways of reaching out to her.

Little did she know, the answer lay hidden within the pages of a story yet to be told, a tale of mystery and intrigue that would forever alter the course of her destiny.

The air once again made strange patterns.

The wind quieted. The curtains settled.

The night remained still.

But something had begun.

Something unseen. Something waiting.

❖

CHAPTER 10

NAACAL SECRET

"Stone speaks volumes when carved."

"Wake up! Wake up!"

Aruzhla groaned as someone shook her. Her eyes fluttered open to see her sister, Dindubi, standing over her, looking frantic.

"It's noon! Get up!"

Aruzhla sat up slowly, rubbing her eyes, and felt something odd against her cheek. She pulled it away—a leaf.
Her breath caught.

The same leaf—the golden-brown veins, the curled edges, the one she had placed at the temple last evening.

But how?

Before she could process it, Dindubi grabbed her wrist. "Aru! What's wrong with everyone today? Why is the whole house still asleep?"

Aruzhla blinked in confusion. "What do you mean?"

"I mean, it's noon, and everyone is still in bed! Even Mum! She always wakes up before sunrise, but today—nothing! I only found out because I got home from my night shift and the whole house was silent. It felt... strange."

A chill ran down Aruzhla's spine. Her mother never overslept. Ever.

Dindubi continued, her voice urgent. "Then I came to wake you. But the real reason I woke you up is this—"

She grabbed Aruzhla's phone from the bedside table. The screen was flashing.

Missed calls. Messages. Dozens of them.

Something was wrong.
Aruzhla's pulse quickened as she reached for her phone. The wind outside howled suddenly, rattling the windows. The leaf in her hand trembled.

Something was very, very wrong.

Aruzhla glanced at her sister, suspicion creeping into her voice. "Wait… where were you all night?"

Dindubi frowned, as if realizing something herself. "What do you mean? I was at Dad's office."

"Dad's office?" Aruzhla's confusion deepened. "I thought you came home from tuition yesterday? Didn't you sleep here?"

"No!" Dindubi shook her head. "Dad called me in the evening. He asked me to bring his treasure box from home to his office."

Aruzhla's breath hitched. "The treasure box?"

Their father's most guarded possession. A heavy, wooden chest, locked tight, always kept hidden behind a secret door in his bedroom wall. Nobody was ever allowed to touch it. Not even their mother.

"Why would he suddenly ask for it?" Aruzhla whispered, her voice barely above a breath.

Dindubi shook her head, her face tense. "I don't know… but something felt strange. He sounded… different. Rushed. Nervous."

Aruzhla's heart pounded. Dad never let anyone near that box. And now, for the first time, he had sent for it?

She looked down at the leaf still in her hand. A sudden gust of wind from the open window sent shivers through her spine.

Something was wrong. Terribly wrong.

"What's in that box, Dindu?" Aruzhla asked, her voice trembling.

The room fell into silence. Outside, the wind howled louder.

"Well, Dad said I shouldn't tell anyone."

After a bit of hesitation, "I trust you. Please don't tell anyone about this, okay? Else, Dad will be mad at me." Dindubi showed a bit of hesitance. She couldn't hide it from her sister of course! It was one of their girl-thingy rules.

"Sure, Sure, you can trust me. Now tell me, what was inside that box?" Aruzhla enquired further.

Dindubi hesitated again for a moment, then sighed. "Honestly… I was just as curious as you. When I bought the box, even I wanted to know what was inside it. And then…" She paused, her eyes glimmering with wonder. "It was amazing, Aru. I never expected this."

Aruzhla leaned in. "What was inside?"

Dindubi's voice lowered as if sharing a secret meant only for them. "At first, it was just a bunch of old papers. I thought it was boring. But then Dad told me to switch off the lights."
Aruzhla's breath caught. "And?"

"And then… the papers started glowing."

A strange chill ran down Aruzhla's spine.
"Glowing?" she repeated, her mind struggling to make sense of it. "I can't believe it, you must be joking. How can a paper glow?"

"Yes!" Dindubi nodded, her eyes wide with excitement.

"They were not ordinary papers; they were resistant to water… Kind of like a litmus test, I thought at first."

"It was like they were alive! I stood there, completely mesmerized, watching as Dad carefully ran his fingers over them. Strange symbols appeared on the surface like hidden writing coming to life in the dark. And that's when he showed me the stones in the treasure box and told me…"

"Told you what?" Aruzhla pressed, barely able to contain herself.

Dindubi's lips parted, her voice barely above a whisper.

"These were the Naacal Tablets."

Aruzhla froze. "The what?"

"The Naacal Tablets," Dindubi repeated. "Dad said they are
the last surviving records of an ancient civilization... a
civilization that existed before all known history."

Aruzhla felt a cold wave wash over her. Ancient civilization?
Before all known history?

"But that's not all," Dindubi continued, her expression
turning serious. "He said the writing on those tablets—when
read the right way—holds secrets about a lost world... a
world that vanished thousands of years ago."

A lost world. Hidden knowledge. And her father had been
studying it in secret.

"Wait, explain me from the beginning. I am not able to
understand," demanded Aruzhla.

Dindubi then spoke slowly. "Okay! First, we turned off the
lights. He picked one of the papers from the treasure box—he
placed it inside a small aquarium."

Aruzhla's breath caught. "The office aquarium?"

Dindubi nodded. "Yes! The one he never let us go near."

Aruzhla shivered. Their father had always been protective of
that aquarium as if it held something more than just fish.

"What happened next?" she whispered.

Dindubi's voice dropped lower. "The moment the litmus-type paper touched the water, the fish inside started circling it. Not randomly—in a pattern. Like they were following something. It was amazing, the fishes were communicating something to us."

Aruzhla's grip tightened on the bedsheet. "And the symbols?"

"That's when the paper started glowing."

Dindubi's eyes darkened as she continued. "New symbols appeared on the glowing paper. Strange, intricate markings.

Dad didn't waste a second—he copied them down into his notebook, then carefully searched for those symbols in the small stones."

Aruzhla felt an eerie shiver run down her spine.
"But why?" she asked, barely able to form the words.

Dindubi exhaled. "That's exactly what I asked him."

A brief silence hung between them.
"And what did he say?" Aruzhla pressed.

Dindubi swallowed hard. "He said... the stones were the key to something much bigger. And each stone had many symbols, they were very tiny. We struggled a lot to find the right stone containing the exact symbols."

Aruzhla scoffed. "Wait, wait, wait—are you telling me a movie story?"

Dindubi rolled her eyes and gave her a sisterly knock on the forehead with her fist. "Will you ever listen fully before making jokes?"

Aruzhla grinned, rubbing her head. "Alright, alright. Continue!"

Dindubi crossed her arms. "As I was saying—every time the fish circled the paper, new symbols appeared. Not the same ones. Different colors, different shapes, each time something new. And Dad? He carefully noted down every detail."

"And then?" Aruzhla prompted, now genuinely intrigued.

"Then he searched for that symbol in his collection of stones. If he didn't find one, he carved every single one of those symbols onto a separate stone from the treasure box. It took him hours. Five, to be exact."

Aruzhla's eyebrows shot up. "Five hours? Just searching and carving?"

"Yes. He said that perfection is the key to decoding them. And then came the really strange part," Dindubi continued.

Aruzhla leaned forward. "What did he do?"

Dindubi's voice dropped lower. "He took the stone matching the first symbol, and hit it against the second. Then he hit the second against the third. And so on."

Aruzhla frowned. "What? Like knocking them together?"

"Like gentle knocking. But it wasn't random."

"What do you mean?"

Dindubi's eyes glowed with excitement. "Each time he hit one stone against the next, a different sound was produced. It was rhythmic, almost like a pattern. He recorded all of it on his device."

Aruzhla's mind was racing. "Wait... are you saying these symbols actually make sounds when struck together?"

"Yes!" Dindubi said, her voice rising. "And Dad thinks it's some kind of message. A sound language from the ancient civilization that had to be deciphered."

Aruzhla felt a chill run down her spine.
"A language made from the sounds of stones..." she murmured. "That's... kind of incredible."

Dindubi nodded. "And terrifying."

Aruzhla swallowed hard. "Why terrifying?"

Dindubi's expression darkened.

"Because the last sound—the very last one—did something neither of us expected."

Dindubi took a deep breath, her eyes filled with something between awe and fear. "It was a coded message," she whispered.

Aruzhla's chest tightened. "Coded? What did it say?"

Dindubi hesitated. "Dad spent hours decoding it. And when he finally pieced it together, he looked… disturbed. He said the world is in danger. That a prophecy had been revealed."

Aruzhla's heartbeat quickened. "What prophecy? What danger? Who—how?"

Dindubi exhaled sharply. "The message said… the world will descend into chaos very soon. People will lose their minds. And then…" she hesitated before saying, "an old Egyptian goddess, Zhautren, has escaped."

Aruzhla blinked. "What? Who?"

Dindubi shook her head. "I have no idea. I've never heard of any Zhautren before. But Dad—he looked like he knew. He didn't explain, just kept muttering under his breath, flipping through pages of his old research notes. He barely spoke to me after that. Just kept writing."

Aruzhla sat up straight. "What was the last message? You said it was incredible?"

Dindubi's eyes gleamed. "Yes. The colors… they were unreal. Unlike anything I've ever seen before. They weren't just glowing—they were… alive. It felt like they were moving, shifting, breathing."

"They were made of symbols. The gigantic Sun… the planets in a line… fast supersonic rays of light… aliens… and a man holding the sun in his palms… and suddenly…"

Aruzhla's skin prickled. "And suddenly what?"

"Suddenly, the symbols inverted to reveal…."

"Reveal what?" Aruzhla couldn't contain herself.
Dindubi lowered her voice. "Dad said it should never be spoken aloud. That the last message can only be written in water."

Aruzhla frowned. "What does that even mean?"

Without answering, Dindubi grabbed a piece of paper and scrawled something across it.
K A L K H A M - she wrote.

The world outside felt different now. Like something invisible had shifted.

"Aru," Dindubi said, pulling her out of her thoughts, "whatever is happening… Dad knew it was coming. That's why he needed the tablets."

Aruzhla swallowed hard. The pieces were coming together. But the real question was—
What was their father hiding? Why? Who is this Zhautren?

"What is this KALKHAM?" She muttered.

"Ssh! Don't speak of it. It's the secret of secrets," Dindubi reminded her.

Both of them kept staring at the paper. The moment the ink settled, a chill filled the air. The air in the room blew the leaf again violently.

And then— Aruzhla's phone vibrated violently in her hand. "Low battery," the screen flashed. Then, without warning— blackout. Her phone powered off.

A heavy silence filled the room.

Dindubi wondered, "What was that?"
Aruzhla still staring at the paper, "I… I don't know."

CHAPTER 11

THE MISSING LEAF

"When logic fails, nature whispers the answer."

Aruzhla sat on the edge of her bed, staring at the golden-brown leaf that was still stuck to her face. She peeled it off, holding it between her fingers. Its delicate veins shimmered faintly under the soft daylight. She had no idea how or why it had followed her, but there it was—again.

"Aruzhla!" Dindubi gasped, snatching the leaf from her hand. "Look at this! This is no ordinary leaf. Where did you even get this?" Her eyes widened as she examined it.

Aruzhla sighed, rubbing her temples. "I don't know. It was just… there. The wind brought it in, and I found it on my face again this morning."

"Again?" Dindubi's excitement grew. "What do you mean again?"

Aruzhla explained everything: the strong winds at the

temple, the sadhu wearing a turban adorned with peacock feathers who watched her, and the strange way the leaf kept returning to her.

"And now, this morning, it was on my face again. What does it even mean?" Aruzhla questioned, more to herself than to her sister.

Dindubi grinned. "It could mean something huge! Maybe it's a sign! Maybe—"

"Oh, come on! It's just a leaf," Aruzhla interrupted, shaking her head. "You're acting like this is some ancient prophecy or something."

Dindubi folded her arms. "And what if it is? Think about it. Why would it follow you? Why from the temple? And why land on your face while you're sleeping? That's too much of a coincidence."

Aruzhla let out a deep breath. "I think I'm just stressed. Work has been crazy, and things have been strange these past two days. The world itself feels… different."

"What do you mean?" Dindubi asked, her curiosity deepening.

Aruzhla leaned back. "It's all over the news. There are reports of strange events happening everywhere—animals acting weird, birds migrating the wrong way, people suddenly losing their memory. And deep down, I feel uneasy, like something is shifting, something big."

Dindubi frowned. "Aruzhla… what if nature is trying to tell you something?"

"What if the leaf is a message?"

"What if you're connected to whatever is happening?"

Aruzhla scoffed. "Oh, please! The only connection I have, is a pile of unfinished office work." She shook her head. "You're reading too much into this."

Just as she finished speaking, a strong gust of wind howled outside. Both sisters turned to the window. The curtains fluttered wildly. The air carried an eerie whisper.

Dindubi smirked. "See? I don't think so."

Aruzhla rolled her eyes but said nothing.

Dindubi narrowed her eyes. "Something strange is happening around you, Aruzhla. You need to be receptive to the message. The wind, the leaf…and then this Naacal stone message… it's not a coincidence."

"Something is happening around you" she finished.

Aruzhla crossed her arms. "Maybe the sadhu wasn't happy that I placed the banyan leaf in front of the snake idol. Maybe he thought it was an insult to the idol, and that's why he walked back to my room and threw the leaf inside through the window." She nodded, trying to convince herself. "That's a much more logical explanation."

Dindubi sighed. "You really think a sadhu walked miles just to return a leaf?"

Aruzhla shrugged, but deep down, she wasn't so sure.

Something about the way the wind carried the leaf unsettled her. But her rational mind pushed those thoughts aside. She had spent years working in the news, analyzing stories, and breaking things down to their core. In her world, nothing was divine, nothing was beyond human explanation. Everything could be traced back to logic, to human intervention. It was hard to believe that nature could send a message.

Yet, as she sat there, holding the leaf, something in her heart whispered otherwise.

Dindubi placed a hand on her shoulder. "Sometimes, we have to look deeper, Aruzhla. Sometimes, nature speaks in ways we don't understand. And when something doesn't feel right, we need to pay attention."

Aruzhla said nothing.

They sat and talked for almost three hours, the conversation shifting between disbelief and growing concern. Dindubi kept circling back to the leaf, convinced that it was more than just a coincidence. Aruzhla, despite her skepticism, couldn't completely shake the feeling that something was truly wrong.

Then—
Knock. Knock. Knock.

Rapid knocking echoed through the house, urgent and hurried.

Both sisters exchanged glances and rushed to the door. Standing there, drenched in sweat, gripping a bag tightly against his chest, was their father—Brahmar.

"Dad?" Aruzhla stepped forward. "What happened?"
Brahmar's eyes darted around. "We need to leave. Now!" His voice was low, urgent, almost trembling. He pushed past them and hurried inside, his breathing heavy.

Dindubi followed, concern etched on her face. "Dad, what's going on? You've been up all night working on the Naacal stones. Did you decode anything new?"

But Brahmar didn't respond. Instead, he rushed to his room, muttering, "It's not safe anymore."

Dindubi raised her voice. "Dad! What's wrong? You're scaring us!"

Brahmar finally stopped and turned to them, his face pale. "I was being watched. At the office, I felt them outside. Dark figures, staring, waiting. They know about the stones."

Aruzhla's heart pounded. "Who? Who's watching you?"

"I don't know! But I couldn't stay there. I had to bring the treasure box home. I had to protect it!"

Dindubi suddenly looked at Aruzhla's leaf again, realization dawning. "Aruzhla… the leaf was telling you something! It was following you. It was warning you that you're being followed!"

A shiver ran down Aruzhla's spine. "The leaf… a warning?"

Brahmar turned sharply. "Did you say leaf?"

He grabbed Dindubi's shoulders, his eyes full of urgency. "You just saved us! The leaf—thank you, dear!"

Brahmar was hiding many secret and rare items in his room. Hearing the word 'leaf' from Dindubi, reminded him of something that he had kept in his secret vault.

Before they could ask him what he meant, Brahmar rushed to his secret compartment behind the bedroom wall.

"I need to find it before we leave. The missing Nadi leaf. It's the only solution to everything happening right now."

He frantically searched through the items, his face growing more anxious by the second.

Then, his gaze shifted to the bed where Poorna and Jittu were still asleep. His eyes widened in shock.

"Why are they still sleeping? It's noon!" he exclaimed, stepping closer to them. "No wonder… the prophecy has already begun. It will soon reveal itself to the whole world!"

His worry deepened. He rushed to Dindubi. "Wake them up! Quickly!" he ordered while continuing his search for the Nadi leaf.

Dindubi hurried over to her mother, shaking her gently. "Mum! Wake up! Dad says we have to leave!"

Poorna stirred, opening her eyes groggily, followed by Jittu, who yawned and stretched. "What's going on?" Poorna asked, rubbing her eyes.

Before Brahmar could reply, a loud knock echoed through the house.

Bang! Bang! Bang!

Everyone froze.

Aruzhla's stomach tightened. "Who… who is that?"

The knocking grew more aggressive, sending a chill down their spines.

Brahmar's fingers trembled as he pulled out a single palm leaf with faded inscriptions. "The missing Nadi leaf… it contains the answer."

The doorknob turned, and a cold chill filled the air.

Whoever—or whatever—was outside… was trying to get in.

CHAPTER 12

DANCE OF PEACOCKS

"You discover yourself in the journey, not in the goal."

Brahmar knew this was the moment. He had to act fast. The intruders were inside the house. His family's safety depended on what he did next.

"Come inside my room, now!" he whispered urgently, locking the door behind them.

The room was silent except for their anxious breathing. Jittu, the youngest, watched as Brahmar bent down and slid a hidden tile under the bed.

A deep rumbling sound followed, revealing a dark, narrow staircase leading underground.

"A secret tunnel under the bed?" Jittu gasped. No one had ever imagined something like this existed in their house. Even the housemaids who regularly cleaned their rooms had no clue.

"There's no time for questions. Get in!" Brahmar ordered.

One by one, they climbed into the tunnel. Brahmar was the last to enter, sealing the tile behind him. Darkness swallowed them whole.

Above them, the sound of footsteps grew louder. The intruders were inside the room.

"Dad, where does this lead?" whispered Aruzhla, trying not to let panic creep into her voice.

"Shh!" Brahmar gestured for silence, his finger to his lips. He led the way through the narrow, damp tunnel.

They moved slowly, feeling their way forward until, finally, after what felt like an eternity, they emerged into an abandoned elevator shaft two streets away. The old lift was rusted and broken—no one paid attention to this place anymore.

"We're safe for now. Follow me," Brahmar said, leading them across the road toward a bus station. A large interstate bus was refueling at a petrol station nearby. Without hesitation, they boarded.

As the bus pulled away, Brahmar finally allowed himself to exhale. His treasure chest was still with him, tightly gripped in his hands. But now, all eyes were on him. Aruzhla and

Dindubi were curious. Poorna and Jittu were shocked. No one knew what was happening. They deserved answers.

"Dad," Aruzhla said, her voice steady, "what is going on?"

Brahmar nodded. "I owe you all an explanation. It starts with something very few people know about—the Theosophical Society."

"The Theosophical Society," Brahmar began, "It's an organization dedicated to studying ancient civilizations, their scriptures, and the artifacts they left behind. We don't rely on myths or blind beliefs."

"We search for real evidence of humanity's origins and evolution." He spoke softly now so as not to get attention from the others in the bus.

Jittu's eyes widened. "So, like archaeologists?"

"Something like that," Brahmar nodded. "But we go beyond what's accepted as history. Many of our discoveries have no scientific explanations."

"Like what?" Dindubi asked, intrigued.

Brahmar smiled. "Like the Naacal tablets, the Lemurian crystals, the Aboriginal Dreamtime sites in Australia, and the Nadi leaves from India."

Aruzhla and Dindubi looked at each other. By now, they had some idea about the Naacal tablets. But this was different. Their father wasn't just talking about these things—he had been part of something bigger.

"What are Nadi leaves?" asked Dindubi.

Brahmar's face darkened, as if he were reliving something from his past. "It's time you knew," he said. "It all started many years ago—when I met Babaji."

"My Journey to Mayiladuthurai" Brahmar leaned back in his seat, his voice shifting into the rhythm of a storyteller.

"Almost 15 years ago, I was curious about the world. I wanted to know where we came from, and what hidden knowledge our ancestors left behind. And one occasion, I got an assignment on the study of thumb imprints. It is said that every human on earth in the past, present or the future has unique thumbprints. That's when I met Babaji. He was a knowledgeable man, who had travelled through secret places in the forests in south India—ones even historians and scientists had never set foot in."

One day, Babaji invited me to a sacred place— Mayiladuthurai.

"Mayiladuthurai?" Jittu repeated. "What's so special about it?"

Brahmar's eyes twinkled. "It's the land where peacocks danced by the fire—a rare celestial ritual."

"In ancient times," he continued, "a goddess once took the form of a peacock and performed a divine dance here. That's how the town got its name. But beyond the myths, Mayiladuthurai hides something even more mysterious—the Nadi leaves."

"The Mystery of Nadi Leaves?" Asked Aruzhla.

"What is that? How can a leaf be mysterious? It sounds so silly. I see leaves on so many trees around. Isn't this sounding silly to all of you?" asked Jittu acting intelligent for his age.

"Jittu, this is not your typical shaktimaan story to amaze you. So, please—be quiet!" Aruzhla silenced him.

"Nadi leaves," Brahmar explained, "are ancient palm-leaf manuscripts written by Indian sages thousands of years ago."

"They contain the past, present, and future of every human being. They were written in an old Tamil script and preserved with peacock oil to last centuries."

Aruzhla's jaw dropped. "So, someone wrote about us thousands of years ago?"

"Not about us, but our life journey in different bodies," Brahmar corrected.

"What's the difference?" Asked Dindubi.

 "These sages, called Rishis, had the ability to see beyond time. They wrote down everyone's destiny on these leaves."

"The writings don't just explain about human life. They also explain about all your previous lives in detail. As in, which place and time you were born, etc. Not just on earth, but on different planets and different forms…"

"But how did they know?" Jittu asked, doubtful.

"No one knows for sure," Brahmar admitted. "Some believe they meditated so deeply that they could access a universal consciousness—like a giant memory of the universe."

"Giant memory?" Asked Jittu. "Wow! Maybe he was Shaktimaan's dad" said Jittu.

"Stop it Jittu! It's not funny!" said Dindubi.

"One night, Babaji and I went deep into the forests of Mayiladuthurai," Brahmar continued. "We had heard that on one special moon, the whispers of peacocks meant a great spectacle treat for eyes as hundreds of peacocks gather and perform a dance. So we went deep into the forest. Slowly the dusk set in.. and we happened to see some lights from far away. We came closer to realize there was a secret tribal fire ritual going on—the Dance of Peacocks. Few had ever seen it.

It was said that this dance opened pathways to a lost land—
Kumari Kandam."

"Kumari Kandam?" Dindubi frowned. "Isn't that just a myth?"

"No," Brahmar said gravely. "It is real—rather, I should say,
alive. But very few know the truth."

The bus rumbled along the highway as Brahmar continued
his story. He described the fire-lit clearing deep in the forest,
the tribal dancers moving in hypnotic circles, their feet
creating patterns in the dirt. The flames rose higher, casting
shadows that flickered like spirits. It was a dance older than
history itself.

"The peacock created ripples, transcending layers of
memories imprinted upon it and forming a 'Darshan'—that's
what the tribe called these visions," he explained.

Babaji had once told him that this dance was not just a ritual
—it was a gateway.

"I remember how curious Babaji always was. He wanted to
understand the science behind the vision, the Darshan, and
he inquired about them with the tribal chief."

The chief had explained that the special moon and the sacred
waters guided the peacock to reach the peak of its life
experience, allowing it to transcend time. And when that
happened, the moonlight and water united in celebration of

life itself. "That experience creates a union, the union creates a form, the form creates ripples on matter, and finally matter merges in time and projects a vision. That," the chief had said, "is the true meaning of Darshan."

"It was breathtaking. The fire ritual was incredibly rare." Brahmar recalled.

"Why is it rare? Can't it be performed more frequently? Is there some special significance to the fire ritual?" Aruzhla asked.

"Yes, it is very rare—both to perform the ritual and to witness it. In a way, it was obtained from pure light beings through the language of the dead."

"Darshan, or the visions, are meant only for a select few. It is predestined, much like what is written in the peacock Nadi leaves. Each Darshan holds a great revelation, almost like the knowledge of a billion library books condensed into a single vision—past, present, and future intertwined in one unified experience.

Remember, a famous scientist spent his entire life searching for the single law that governs the universe. That is exactly what this vision reveals. The Darshan... it allows one to zoom into any moment in the journey of the universe, as if you are flowing through its very veins, witnessing its timeless dance." "That's why the ritual is called a dance—the Dance of Peacocks," he concluded.

The lost civilization of Kumari Kandam was hidden in layers of time, protected by those who still carried its ancient wisdom.

"That night was long, we met them after the dance and they were welcoming. They did not harm us. Good old days. It's only now that people don't trust each other. To keep the story short, a tribal elder handed me a Nadi leaf—one that had my name written on it."

"Your Nadi leaf? Your name already written in it?" asked Aruzhla shocked.

"Yes, it was pre-written. The leaf imprints even detailed my past and present identities—the different forms of life I have lived, my current human existence, and every detail about my family with perfect accuracy. It also mentioned where and when I would meet your mother, how many children we would have, and so on," he said with a smile.

"Even Babaji was astonished to learn about his past, present, and future. We had long discussions about how he would go incognito in the times to come."

"Nature is like a dream—you never truly know what is real and what is not. Life, on the other hand, feels like reality, yet you can never be certain what is a dream and what is not," Brahmar said thoughtfully, reminiscing about those magical moments of his life.

"Impossible, this is beyond science," said Dindubi.

"True, welcome to theosophical society. We go where science can't reach, where human consciousness alone can reach." He explained.

"It contained secrets about my life, my purpose, and a prophecy about a hidden treasure that could change the world."

"This leaf," Brahmar said, pointing to his treasure chest, "was part of the Kumari Kandam records. It is said to hold the answers to humanity's greatest questions. That is why I had to protect it at all costs."

"Even after studying billions of books, one may still not find the truth. But this—" he pointed to the Nadi leaf—"contains all the answers."

A heavy silence settled over them. Just then, the bus screeched to a halt. The bus driver shouted, "Who is blocking the bus?"

A group of masked men stormed in, guns drawn.

Brahmar froze. How had they found them?

Dindubi's sharp eyes darted around. Something wasn't right. Then it hit her.

"It's your office phone!" she whispered urgently to Aruzhla. "Your boss—he's tracking us!"

A cold chill ran down Aruzhla's spine. Bhaskar, her boss, had given her a branded office phone to stay connected on her day off. When she had discussed the Naacal stones with Dindubi earlier, the phone must have accidentally connected. Bhaskar had overheard everything.

Dindubi's gaze locked onto the man holding the gun. A scorpion tattoo on his wrist. Recognition struck her like lightning.

"That tattoo…" she whispered. "Bhaskar's men."

The masked leader stepped forward. "Get down. All five of you."

"Step out! Now!" the masked man barked.

Brahmar knew there was no way out. He glanced at his children. Aruzhla, Dindubi, and Jittu sat frozen, their faces pale with fear. Poorna, his wife, clutched his arm, her eyes filled with silent terror.

"Do exactly as they say. Stay close to me," Brahmar whispered, then turned to the driver. "Go. Drive away. This is not your fight."

The driver hesitated but nodded. As soon as the family of five stepped off the bus, the vehicle pulled away, leaving them alone on the deserted road. The thick jungle surrounded them, the air heavy with the scent of damp earth and leaves. The winding, zig-zag path suggested they were somewhere deep in the forests near Rameshwaram.

The men pointed their guns. "Into the car. Move!"

A black SUV stood by the side of the road, its engine running. The men gestured for them to get inside. The cold metal of the gun against their backs made it clear there was no room for argument.

Nature is man's untapped wisdom. When nature takes control, nothing—absolutely nothing—can stop it, not even a man's will.

As they walked, the wind picked up. Dry leaves swirled around their feet. Aruzhla noticed it immediately.

The wind had blown like this yesterday too—first stirring dust, then making banyan leaves dance, then catching the sharp, knowing gaze of a sadhu sitting by the roadside. She had ignored it then. But now, standing here, forced at gunpoint, she felt something strange. Was this a sign? Was her sister right about the universe speaking to them?

Then, the wind blew again, stronger this time. The leaves on the ground lifted, spiraling in a chaotic dance. One of the masked men cursed under his breath, rubbing his eyes as dust flew into them.

Aruzhla's mind clicked into place. This was the moment. Without thinking, she bent down, grabbed a handful of sand, and in one swift motion, flung it into the masked men's faces.

"Ahh!" One of them shouted, stumbling backward, his hands flying to his burning eyes.

The other barely had time to react before Dindubi and Jittu did the same, scooping up dirt and hurling it at their attackers.

Jittu giggled, finding it oddly fun. "This is like our sand fight at the beach!"

The masked men flailed, momentarily blinded, their fingers gripping the triggers but unable to aim.

Brahmar didn't waste a second. He lunged forward, knocking the gun from the first man's hand. With the reflexes of a decent fighter, he grabbed the weapon and turned it on them.

Bang! Bang!
He fired two shots at their feet, making them stumble back and collapse onto the ground, groaning in pain.

"Run!" Brahmar ordered.

They dashed towards the SUV. Brahmar jumped into the driver's seat, slamming the door shut. The engine was already running. He hit the gas, and the car sped off, tyres screeching against the dirt road.

"Are they following us?" Dindubi asked breathlessly, twisting in her seat.

"Not yet," Aruzhla said, watching the two figures in the rearview mirror. "But—" before she could finish, a sharp sound rang through the air. A gunshot.

Crack! A bullet struck the rear tyre.

Brahmar's grip on the wheel tightened as the car swerved violently. He struggled to control it, but the road was too uneven, the turns too sharp. The steering wheel fought against him.

"Hold on!" he shouted.

The car veered dangerously to the side, teetering on the edge of the mountain road. Then, as if in slow motion, the ground beneath them vanished.

The SUV tumbled off the cliff.

Aruzhla screamed as they plunged downward, flipping and rolling, the world outside a blur of trees and sky.

Branches snapped against the car, windows shattered, and the metal frame groaned as it twisted under the force of impact.

Down, down, down they fell, until finally—the crash.

The vehicle hit the ground with a bone-rattling thud, rolling one last time before coming to a stop.
Silence.

A bird cawed in the distance. Leaves rustled in the wind. The dust settled around them.

Then—a cough.

Brahmar groaned, his head pounding. His vision blurred, but he could see movement beside him. Dindubi was clutching her arm, wincing. Jittu groaned but was already sitting up. Aruzhla blinked rapidly, trying to focus. Poorna gasped for breath, holding her side.

They were hurt. Scraped, bruised, maybe even bleeding—but they were alive. A slow, painful realization crept over them. They had survived.

Brahmar took a deep breath, his mind racing. If the intruders came looking, they needed to believe the family had perished in the crash.

He glanced around and saw dry logs scattered nearby. Without wasting a moment, he gathered them and stacked them near the car's crumpled engine.

Then, reaching into his pocket, he pulled out his lighter.

Click.

A small flame flickered to life. He held it to the logs, watching as the fire caught, crackling and spreading to the car's metal frame. The flames licked the shattered windshield, curling into the air like ghostly fingers.

"Come on," he whispered to his family.

"We need to go. Now."

The fire grew, swallowing the wreckage. If the intruders followed their trail, they would only find a burning shell, charred and unrecognizable. They would believe no one could have survived.

Brahmar took one last look at the flames before leading his family into the dense jungle, disappearing into the shadows.

❖

CHAPTER 13

UNSEEN CONNECTIONS

"What you seek will seek you too, if only you can see."

Kalyan sat on the front steps of the old house, running his fingers through the dust that had settled over the years.

This was his grandfather's home, once built with care by Babaji and his father, Manidhar. But now, it was abandoned— forgotten by time, overtaken by silence. The walls, cracked and faded, whispered stories of the past. The wooden beams creaked with every gust of wind, and the surrounding wilderness seemed to inch closer every day, reclaiming the land as its own.

It had been two days since he and his mother, Mandira, had arrived. Two days of clearing out the dust, cobwebs, and remnants of a life once lived.

Two days of waiting—waiting for Dr. Upen to arrive, waiting for news about the black rose extract he had given to Jenny, Dr. Upen's associate.

Had they administered it to the scientists in a coma in Egypt? Had it worked? The silence was unbearable.

"Mom," Kal called out, breaking the stillness.

Mandira was sweeping the front porch, her tired hands moving in a rhythm. "Why hasn't Dr. Upen come yet? I thought he would contact us by now."

Mandira sighed, pausing for a moment. "I don't know, Kalyan. Maybe things didn't go as planned. Or maybe he's caught up in something. We have no way to know from here."

That was true. They were isolated—no phone signal, no internet, no neighbors they knew. The only person they were expecting was Kal's aunt, who had promised to visit and discuss the next arrangements. Until then, they were alone in this forgotten place.

Kal rested his chin on his palm, deep in thought. "I had a strange dream the night we got here," he said suddenly.

Mandira looked up. "What kind of dream?"

"I was back in that graveyard," Kal said, lowering his voice as if the walls themselves were listening. "The same one where I fell unconscious just nights ago… but this time, something was different. There was a glow—a strange, literal light on one of the graves."

Mandira frowned, listening intently.

"And on the grave, I saw a name… KALKHAM."

Mandira's expression didn't change. She simply shook her head. "It doesn't strike anything to me, Kalyan."

Kal sighed. He had hoped his mother would recognize the name, that she would recall some long-lost family secret or hidden truth. But she simply continued cleaning, brushing away dust as if brushing away the mystery itself.

They continued their work in silence for a while. The abandoned house had years' worth of clutter, and many of the items had rusted beyond repair. Kal helped his mother move an old wooden table to the side of the room. It was heavy, and as he lifted it, he noticed something odd—one of the legs was broken. His grandfather had apparently stuffed papers inside the hollow space to keep it stable.

Curious, Kal pulled a few pieces out. For a moment, his heart raced. Could this be a hidden clue? Some long-forgotten message from Babaji?

But as he unfolded the papers, disappointment washed over him. They were just scraps—old newspaper cuttings, lists of household expenses, nothing significant. He sighed, crumpling one in his hand before tossing it aside.

Mandira noticed his curiosity and chuckled. "Your grandfather was a resourceful man. He would fix things in the most unexpected ways. If something broke, he'd find a way to keep it working."

Kal smiled faintly, eager to keep the conversation going. "Tell me more about him, Mom. How was Babaji in his younger days?"

Mandira continued her work as she spoke. "He was a quiet man, but full of wisdom. He believed in signs and omens, always observing nature closely. He used to say that the wind carries messages, and that the earth listens when we speak. He used to go deep into the jungles and study plants and herbs."

Kal's mind drifted back to the dream, to the name glowing on the grave. Was it all just a coincidence, or was something truly trying to reach out to him?

As the day stretched on, they continued clearing out the house, unaware that the past was beginning to stir once more. And somewhere, beyond the reach of time and reality, something—or someone—was waiting for Kal to listen.

Trying to distract himself, Kal crumpled the old papers into a ball and tossed it against the wall. The impact caused bits of paint to flake off, exposing the aged wood beneath. He frowned. "This place isn't safe unless it's properly renovated," he muttered.

Mandira, watching him, nodded in agreement. "You're right, Kalyan. This house needs a lot of work. We can't live here like this for long. I don't know if your grandpa will indeed turn in — Hope he does soon… Just being optimistic for the night."

Just then, a familiar voice called from outside. Mekhala, Mandira's cousin, had arrived, carrying a cloth-wrapped bundle.

"I brought you both some food," she said with a warm smile.

Kal took the bundle eagerly as Mandira invited Mekhala inside. They sat together and ate a simple, delicious home-cooked meal.

The warmth of the food filled their stomachs, and for a while, the women engaged in light rural chatter. The conversation brought a rare sense of comfort to the otherwise eerie house.

Suddenly, with a faint crackling sound, the single light bulb in the room flickered and went out, plunging them into darkness.

Mekhala sighed. "This house…" she muttered. Then, turning to Mandira, she asked, "Why do you both still insist on staying here? It's not in good condition. Why don't you listen to me and come to my house? You can stay there while we get this place fixed."

Mandira hesitated, looking at Kal. He simply smiled. "No, Aunt Mekhala. I know Babaji will come to see us very soon." His words carried a certainty, recalling the prediction by Rheagor, the mountain spirit from his previous journey.

Mekhala shook her head, though she didn't argue. "Fine, then. But even getting a light bulb will be a hassle now. There are no local shops nearby. I know someone who can get one for you. He's a bit far now, but I'll let him know. He might bring it before midnight."

Mandira nodded. "Thank you, Mekhala. That would be helpful."

Mekhala gathered her things and stood up. "I should get going; it's getting dark, and I have a long walk home. I'll see you tomorrow, and I'll bring food again. I packed enough for your breakfast too."

Kal and Mandira bid her goodbye, watching as she walked off into the dusk. The sky had deepened into shades of purple and blue. Kal felt relieved that she had come early and left before it got too dark. There was something about the night in this old house that made his skin prickle.

As he sat back down in the dimly lit room, waiting for the local man to bring them a new bulb, he couldn't shake the feeling that the night held something more than just shadows.

As the sound of Mekhala's footsteps faded into the distance, Kal and Mandira sat in the dim glow.

 The silence of the abandoned house settled around them, broken only by the occasional chirping of crickets outside.

Mandira sighed, stretching her arms. "It's been a long day," she said. "We should try to get some rest."

Kal nodded but kept his gaze fixed on the front door. Something about Mekhala's words lingered in his mind. She had said a local person might come before midnight. Would he really? And if he did, would he be just a simple villager—or someone else entirely? Would Babaji surprise him? Kal's mind wandered, filled with questions.

"Alright, Mom," he finally said. "You go rest. I'll sit here for a while."

Mandira hesitated but eventually gave him a tired smile.

"Don't stay up too late," she said, patting his head before walking towards the small room where they had set up their bedding.

Kal leaned back against the wooden chair, staring at the broken bulb socket. Determined to stay awake, Kal picked up a stone and began etching letters onto the wall.

Slowly, he carved out the word KALKHAM, letting the rhythmic scraping of the stone keep him alert.

The night deepened, and the house grew colder. Kal found himself dozing off, his head bobbing slightly.

Suddenly— *Tap. Tap. Tap.*
A soft knocking sound.

Kal's eyes flew open. He sat up straight, his heart pounding. The knock was not coming from the front door.

He stood up cautiously, his ears straining. Another sound followed—not a knock this time, but soft footsteps, scuffling against the ground. He turned towards the back of the house, where the noise was coming from.

Slowly, he crept towards the rear door, gripping the handle firmly before pulling it open.

It was still dark, with no lights in the house.

"WHO ARE YOU—-?" Kal asked loudly.

"WHO ARE YOU?" Came the response in return.

To his shock, five shadowy figures stood just beyond the doorway. A family of five—three adults and two children— stared at him, startled by his sudden appearance.

The eldest, a man with a rugged face, stepped forward hesitantly. "We— we thought this house was empty," he said cautiously. "We were just looking for a safe place to rest for the night."

Kal's eyes darted between them in the dim light that filled the room through the cracks in the house and small window openings.

The man's face looked weathered, exhausted. Meanwhile, a younger woman, Dindubi, had already begun looking around suspiciously, as if scanning the house for clues. Her detective-like curiosity made Kal uneasy. Another figure, a young boy, clung to her side. He looked terrified of the darkness, his round, chubby face filled with hunger and uncertainty.

The eldest man, Brahmar, took a deep breath. "We had escaped from kidnappers," he admitted.

"We fell off a cliff trying to escape. We've been walking ever since. We just needed a safe place to stop for the night."

"And this was the only deserted house we could see from afar, surrounded by thick bushes and trees—perfect as a hideout."

Kal's gaze flickered downward. Even in the dark, he could sense from their voices that these people had been through something serious.

His initial hesitation faded. He stepped aside and gestured his approval. "Alright," he said. "You can stay here for the night."

"But who are you? What are you doing in this dark place? Alone?" Asked Dindubi.

"It doesn't matter who I am, but I am not alone," Kal replied. "My Mum is sleeping in the other room."

Just as he finished speaking, a sudden knock came from the front door.

Brahmar tensed up immediately. "They found us," he whispered.

Kal shook his head. "No," he said calmly. "This is someone I was expecting."

The group remained still as Kal walked to the door and opened it. A man stood outside, holding a small paper bag. Without a word, he handed Kal the bag, nodded once, and disappeared into the night.

Kal reached inside and pulled out a new light bulb. He continued his story "Mum and I are staying here for the last two days only with the hope that my grandpa, Babaji will meet us here" he lifted his arm to fit the bulb in the dark.

The room illuminated slowly flicker by flicker, revealing everyone's faces slowly.

The moment the light turned on, Brahmar's expression shifted. His eyes widened in shock. "Did you just say... Babaji?" he asked.

Kal turned to him, confused.
"Yes. BABAJI, my grandfather—"

Brahmar's voice trembled. "You mean the tall, slim, well-built man with a brownish complexion? The Ayurvedic researcher and healer?"

"Yes, but he's much older now. I don't think he'd be as strong as before," Kal said. "How do you know Babaji? I've been searching for him! He left everything behind and disappeared. Do you know where he is?"

Brahmar's eyes lit up with excitement. "Oh yes, I know Babaji!" But then his face turned serious. "But I don't know where he is... unless..." He paused, recalling something from a long-ago conversation with Babaji in the forest.

"Unless what?" Kal asked, leaning forward.

"Unless... The Dance of Peacocks... the Fire Ritual... the message for him. The Naacal tablets—they spoke of this moment. The prophecy is real! I can't believe this is happening!" Brahmar's voice shook as if he had just uncovered a great secret.

Kal frowned. He wasn't sure if he could trust him. He sounded a little… crazy.

Before Kal could react, his eyes locked onto the woman beside him—her face now fully visible—and he recognized her instantly.

"Aruzhla? The famous 'viral' news anchor!" he muttered in disbelief.

The woman, Aruzhla, narrowed her eyes. "Do I know you?" she asked.

Kal hesitated, but before he could answer, she gasped. "Wait—you were the one in the news! The accident… Dr. Upen… the Nobel laureate… he came to bail you out of jail. This happened just days ago… in Bangalore! What are you doing here?"

Her words sent a chill through Kal. He had been in that accident. But how did she end up here as well?

Kal stiffened. Everything—every event of the last few days—was colliding here, in this one room, under this one flickering light.

This couldn't be a coincidence. It was something more. The moment the light fully lit up the room, Brahmar froze in shock. He didn't just see Kal clearly—he saw something behind him.

On the wall… a scribe.

His eyes widened. "This… This can't be!"

KALKHAM

———— K A L K H A M ————

It was the same message he had received the night before after decoding the Naacal tablet symbols.

"It was a strange moment. Everyone looked at each other in shock. Each person had different questions, but at that moment, all of their questions had only one answer—
"This can't be a coincidence."

CHAPTER 14

THE SILENT WHISPER

"Time is Her weaving tool to unfold Her mighty essence."

Meanwhile, at Snake Mountain…

Rahasi stood at the entrance of the ancient temple, her heart heavy with the weight of what was about to unfold.

She felt the earth tremble beneath her as though the mountains themselves were aware of the decision she was about to make.

Her father, the wise and respected chieftain of their Naga tribe, stood behind her, his expression filled with concern.

"My daughter," he said softly, his voice laden with years of wisdom and love.

"You know the risks of this journey. To seek the truth at the Temple of the Serpent is not without peril. The path ahead may take more than just your life, but your very soul. I cannot bear the thought of losing you."

Rahasi turned to face her father, her eyes deep with resolve. She had always known that her journey would lead her to this moment. She had seen the future, the dark forces that would soon engulf the earth, and the only way to stop them lay within the answers she would find on this sacred mountain.

"I know, Father," she whispered, her voice calm despite the turmoil within. "But I must go. For the sake of our people, for the sake of the world, I must seek the wisdom that only Prajothi can provide."

The chieftain nodded slowly, his eyes filled with both pride and sorrow. "Then go, my child. May our ancestors and the spirits of the mountain guide you."

With a final glance at her father, Rahasi stepped forward, entering the temple's ancient, snake-carved doors.

The air grew thick with an energy older than time itself. She walked deeper into the cave, her footsteps echoing through the hollow stone corridors, her heart heavy with anticipation.

Listening to her inner voice, she kept walking through the confusing tunnels of the cave. Finally, she reached the heart of the cavern.

Rahasi knelt beside the sacred water pool, its surface still and serene. She closed her eyes, her senses attuned to the whispers of the unseen. She called out to Prajothi, her voice resonating through the stillness.

"Oh Mother, guide of our people, show yourself," she intoned, but no answer came. She waited in silence, the minutes stretching into an eternity.

Frustration rose within her, and she grasped a leaf from the ground. With deliberate care, she dipped the leaf into the water and wrote her question, her soul laid bare in the flicks: What is Dharma, and how do I know when to act and when to stay silent?

As the words settled upon the surface of the water, the fishes swam closer, circling around her writing. The ripples they created seemed to carry the weight of unseen forces, stirring something deep within her.

Rahasi took a deep breath, letting the quietude fill her being. She sang softly, her voice rising in the still air, her song an offering to the spirits.

"Time is everything I can own. Even the air I breathe, is not mine, nor is the sky nor the fire. To own Time, all that I have is 'Now'." She sang.

Her voice grew stronger, filled with the intensity of her emotion. "You came as my mother, as my father, as my friend, as my enemy. You died as the insect beneath my feet, you came as my guilt, you came as my liberator. You became the sin, and you became the liberator. Now you have become my question... why do you not come as my answer?"

The water rippled in response, and from its depths emerged a figure as luminous as the moonlight—Prajothi, her teacher and guide, her presence both soothing and awe-inspiring. Her form shimmered, made of light and water, and her eyes held the wisdom of the universe. She looked at Rahasi with both kindness and mystery.

"You have called me, daughter of the Naga," Prajothi said, her voice like the soft rustle of leaves in the wind. "And you have asked one of the greatest questions."

Rahasi, kneeling before her, felt a mixture of reverence and fear. "Oh Mother, I seek to understand the path of dharma. I have seen the world unravel, and I have also seen the future of this world. However, I do not know when to act and when to refrain. How do I know when to help, and when not to help? For I feel that both acts are equally weighted in dharma. Even not helping may be a form of helping, and helping may sometimes hinder one's karmic journey."

Prajothi's gaze deepened, as if she could see through Rahasi's very soul. "You have asked of dharma, the eternal law. The path of dharma is not linear, nor is it fixed. It is dynamic, like the flow of a river. It shifts with each moment, depending on the circumstances and the beings involved."

She continued, her voice soothing yet piercing. "To help someone is to act in alignment with their need, but to help them too much, or at the wrong time, can prevent them from fulfilling their own karma. You must understand the balance between what is yours to give and what is not yours to take. What is 'you' and what is not 'you.' Only then can you determine the true nature of help."

Rahasi, her mind swirling with the profound teachings of Prajothi, felt the weight of her questions grow even heavier.

The temple's stillness seemed to echo her inner turmoil. She had just begun to grasp the nature of dharma, yet more questions arose, like ripples in the water that seemed impossible to silence.

"Mother," Rahasi spoke, her voice trembling with the depth of her contemplation. "If dharma is not fixed, why is it so elusive? At times, it feels so tricky and difficult to understand. How can I know when to act and when not to act, when the path seems so uncertain?"

Prajothi's eyes softened, and she regarded Rahasi with a knowing, almost timeless gaze. Slowly, she spoke, her voice like a melody that reached the very soul.

"Dharma, my dear, is not a fixed concept only because it is woven into the very fabric of existence. It is not one law that applies to all, at all times. Each person you intend to help is not just a singular identity. It is the sum of all who came before them. It is the aggregation of their ancestors, their lineage, their individual karma and their aggregated karma… The individual you see before you is an outcome of countless generations, and thus, when you act to help, you are not just influencing this one person; you are interacting with the vast web of actions, both good and bad, that have been passed down through time."

Rahasi listened intently, her mind expanding with the weight of this truth. Prajothi continued, her words flowing with deep wisdom.

"Every karmic act, good or bad, from an ancestor, be it from a moving form or a non-moving form, interacts with the eternal laws of nature, the dance of the solar system, and the cosmic energies that flow through all things. This is indeed the suprasonic waves surrounding our planet. Everything is interconnected—human, animal, insect, plant, land, water, air, sky, time, space, even the stars in the sky."

She paused, allowing the gravity of her words to settle in.

"That is why, sometimes, not helping is as much an act of dharma as helping. When you choose not to act, you allow the system to readjust, to realign itself, so that the karmic flow can continue to evolve. Balance is maintained, and the necessary forces have space to adapt. Sometimes, your interference would disrupt the delicate web of karma that is unfolding."

Rahasi's mind tried to grasp the enormity of what she was being told, but the magnitude was overwhelming. "So, helping or not helping is not just about the individual. It is about something much greater, is it?"

Prajothi nodded. "Exactly. Everything in nature seeks balance—every action, every word, every thought. If you are the reason for balance, you will succeed in your endeavors, for you align yourself with the universal flow. But the moment you become a part of the imbalance, know that you have aligned yourself with failure."

"To help is not always to act; to not help is not always to refuse. It is the intention behind the action, the purpose, and the awareness of the consequences that determine your path."

"That is why Bhāva—intention—is important."

"That is why Rāga—the melody of the cosmic song—is important."

"That is why Tāla—the rhythm, the pulse—is important."

"Together, these three form the very essence of Karma Varsha—the sacred rain of Bharathavarsha."

"In the lands of Bharathavarsha, I myself witnessed a mysterious peacock appear on a special full moon night,

revealing the deepest mysteries of life through a divine dance
—the cosmic dance of intention, melody, and rhythm."

"This dance is known as 'The Dance of Peacocks', the dance of
life itself—where ultimate meaning dissolves into one's root
motive, guiding one to enact their dharma-duty."

"The peacock was an apt form for this revelation, for it is a
creature that embodies the pure joy of existence—expressing
life itself through the art of dance."

"Thus, performing one's dharma, or duty, with a good
intention is more valuable than life itself."

Rahasi felt her heart settle as the wisdom began to seep deep
into her being. She understood, in that moment, that dharma
was not a simple rulebook—it was a living, breathing force
that shifted and morphed with each action, each decision,
and each soul.

"But what about the questions we carry?" Rahasi asked, her
voice filled with wonder.

"What about the answers we seek? Is every question meant to
have an answer?"

Prajothi knew the depth of Rahasi's questions. She was not
merely asking; she was seeking something profoundly deep.

Rahasi was no ordinary child. She was the daughter of the

Naga, born for a great purpose. She already knew the future, yet here she was with questions—not for herself, but for something beyond. It was a quest very deep, not for the weak or distracted. Only this who knows, KNOW!

She was asking these questions, knowing that the answers would impact many things in the future. Rahasi understood this, and even Prajothi knew it. Yet, they maintained their distance, remaining two separate individuals. Sometimes, those who know everything are the weakest. For they understand that nothing is in their control, and yet, they must live with that knowledge and perform their roles.

Prajothi's smile was gentle, almost serene. "Not every question needs an answer, Rahasi. Sometimes, no answer is the answer itself. And sometimes, the answer does not need a question. To go beyond answers, to go beyond questions—that is the essence of a balanced mind. It is the mind that is not disturbed by the need for certainty, the mind that sees beyond the dualities of yes and no, of good and bad. This is the identity of one who is at peace, who exists in harmony with the universe."

"What you see may not be true, but what I see in you is the truth!" Rahasi slowly began to understand the portal's secret key. The same phrase that had once unlocked a dimensional travel portal for Kal, the sun incarnate.

Rahasi stood in silence, the weight of her thoughts pushing her to the edge of understanding, but never quite allowing her to grasp it fully. She had always sought answers, always believed that clarity was the key to wisdom. But now, she saw that true wisdom lay in the acceptance of the unknown, in the willingness to be at peace with uncertainty.

"You helped Kal"— she paused and waited.

Prajothi's voice came, slow and deliberate, each word shaping the very air around them.

"Kal is not just an ordinary human. Many still don't know the true extent of his role in this world. But I can only share this much with you... for now. When one's purpose is pure and actions are genuine, you don't need to go to a temple to find God. God will come to you. Because in that moment, the roles switch—the devotee becomes God, and God becomes the devotee. Kal's mission on Earth is selfless and true. Even the gods must rise to support him. They have no choice. That is the power of karma. A force so strong—yet so few truly understand it."

"One who is on the path of righteousness—his actions speak for him, and he becomes a walking God, while all others remain sleeping Gods. Remember this," she paused.

"The world always looks for a hero, someone to name, someone to praise, someone to follow. But in truth, the hero is insignificant. The hero is merely a symbol, a focal point for the collective longing of the people."

Rahasi's lips parted slightly, but she did not speak. She only listened. "To create a hero, an entire web of unseen forces must work in the shadows—people, efforts, betrayals, sacrifices, broken promises. Blood must be spilled, sins must be committed, and right and wrong must blur into one another. Do you think civilizations rise and fall by the actions of one man or woman? No. It is a tide, an inevitable movement of time. And yet, the world clings to the idea of a single savior."

She paused, allowing the silence to breathe. "Look at all the civilizations that have passed by..." Rahasi's mind swirled.

"The hero was never alone. The hero was never the doer." Prajothi's voice was steady, timeless.

"Dharma, Artha, Kaama, Moksha—they are not four different things. They are four faces of the same coin, shifting with each turn of time. What you call Dharma today, will soon become Artha. What is Artha, will become Kaama. What is Kaama, will dissolve into Moksha. And then the cycle will turn again."

She turned towards Rahasi, her gaze piercing. "Once you truly know this, even the gods become meaningless. Even the self becomes worthless. Do you understand?"

Rahasi inhaled sharply. A shiver ran down her spine.

"Remember this: the stick that helps the blind becomes meaningless the moment sight is restored. So too are the gods. So too are all relationships. So too is the self. So too is this world."

"What exists beyond balance?" Rahasi asked softly, the question hanging in the air like a fleeting dream.

Prajothi's eyes shimmered with the depths of the cosmos as she answered, her voice resonating with the eternal truth. "Everything."

Rahasi's heart fluttered in her chest. "I... I am.. Am I.. Everything?"

Prajothi's smile was radiant, as though she had just unlocked the deepest secret of the universe. "You are everything. The entire universe resides within you, as it resides in all things. You are the sum of your ancestors, your actions, your choices, your thoughts. You are both the question and the answer, the balance and the chaos. And when you understand this, you will know that you are never alone, for the entirety of existence is with you, in every step, in every breath."

"The only thing that stops every life from being who they actually are is they put every effort to become something that they are not... That may look very *small*... but that is *all*."

"Just Be..."
"Just Be..."

"Everything will align itself to serve you, to protect you, to liberate you, to become what you truly are meant to be here." she gave her the secret formula.

Rahasi felt her soul expand, stretching out beyond the confines of her body, touching the very edges of the universe. For the first time, she understood—dharma was not a path to follow, but a dance to be participated in. It was not a question to be answered, but an existence to be experienced.

As Prajothi's form began to dissolve into the ethereal light of the cave, Rahasi stood alone, her heart filled with a newfound clarity. She was not just a daughter of the Naga tribe. She was part of the eternal flow, the cosmic rhythm that moved through all things.

"Remember," Prajothi's voice echoed one last time, "the power of your actions lies not in the act itself, but in the balance it creates. You will always succeed if you are the reason for the balance. You will fail the moment you become part of the imbalance."

This—this—was very important for Rahasi. It sank in deeply, resonating within her. The world was not ready for Rahasi's next plan, and this answer held immense significance.

Rahasi listened intently, the weight of the words sinking into her consciousness. "And how do I know where to draw the line?" she asked, her voice trembling with uncertainty.

Prajothi smiled gently. "In every moment, ask yourself: Is this act mine to do? Does this action align with the greater cosmic order, the flow of the universe? If yes, then act. If not, step back. Even in not acting, you are still part of the divine flow."

Rahasi felt the weight of her power and responsibility settle upon her. "I understand," she whispered.

Prajothi's form began to fade, her light receding into the water. "Remember, Rahasi," she said, her voice now echoing from beyond the veil, "You are allowed to use your occult powers only three times to save humanity. Use them wisely. For each time you act, you shift the course of fate itself. And remember the sacred promise—four lives must always guard a newborn human soul. The life of the birth bird, the birth animal, the birth spirit, and the birth human friend soul." Rahasi's heart swelled with understanding, the enormity of her role dawning upon her. She rose to her feet, ready to face the world that awaited her, knowing that the balance between dharma, Artha, Kaama and Moksha, was now within her grasp.

As she stepped back from the water, a voice echoed in her mind, the voice of the portal itself: "Your path is now set. Choose wisely, for the balance of all things hangs in the balance. You will use your powers three times. Your first choice awaits."

With a final look at the temple's entrance, Rahasi stepped out into the world, her soul fortified with the ancient wisdom she had uncovered, her heart determined to side with Kalyan and protect humanity's fragile future.

And as the snake mountain whispered behind her, she knew her journey was just beginning.

With great determination, fully focused, with no other options left, no questions left, no answers left, no more confusion clouding her identity anymore, she looked at the world. With compassion and grace, she sat in deep meditation now.

"Just Be" she recalled and deep she went into the inner worlds…

Far far away in her vision, she saw great grand white mountains… snowing everywhere around..

A small gathering of wise men put a question to a central mystic figure who sat as thought perfection embodiment.

"Aadi.. the very life is in danger… An alien life named 'Q' has overtaken the minds of the people on earth. He is about to overshadow a great cosmic alignment in a few moon days. Shall we destroy him in an instant? We need your permission. Please let us know what is right?" asked one wise man.

The central mystic, with a light body, smiled. "Someone has accessed this space… the KALKHAM space…" And, listening to our conversation, he added.

"TIME (KAAL) should not stop on Earth, but..."

"Indeed, when a secret is broken, it is no longer a secret. But when a secret reveals by its own will, it remains intact and continues to be a secret. I grant permission only to this secret —the grand secret—RAHASI." He smiled. The central mystic knew that Rahasi had accessed their space through her first occult powers.

After a moment, Rahasi opened her eyes and came out of her deep meditation. She had just accessed the multi-dimensional parallel and unparallel inaccessible space of KALKHAM. For the first time, it was unlocked on earth by a mere mortal - RAHASI. Her very meaning was "Rahasya" or the Secret. That was the moment she realized the meaning behind her name. The daughter of Naga had been named by Prajoti herself in the past, a name that held more weight than she had ever understood before.

"Just Be" had worked. She knew what to do now.

She once again closed her eyes and went deep into meditation again accessing her inner worlds.

Just breathing "SOH..HAM..." she used her inner senses guided by her will to switch her to jump between inner worlds. After all, she was the daughter of the Naga and was fully trained in more than sixty qualities of human life.

She knew the perfect ways to now access her inner fire along the spine. She didn't need a physical world to communicate to Prajothi again. Just by her inner access she could tap onto her wisdom remotely.

Rahasi's body felt impossibly heavy, yet her mind was weightless, as though she were both sinking into the earth and floating beyond time. Her breath came short, not in fear, but in the overwhelming realization that had just been pitched into her very soul.

She had always sought answers. But now, she was beginning to see that the weight of the truth was far greater than the weight of ignorance.

Prajothi stood before her in her inner vision, radiant and still, the eternal witness to the unfolding of drama on earth and beyond. The cave seemed smaller now, not because it had changed, but because Rahasi had expanded.

The worlds sank into Rahasi's bones. Everything—every idea, every identity—was temporary. Even the self she clung to would one day be discarded like an old garment.

She journeyed along the veins of the universe, and for just one moment, she saw a subtle feminine energy appear. She swallowed, feeling her lips dry. Then, almost in a whisper, she asked, "Who is this feminine? What makes her so powerful?"

"Your questions will never end and so will the answers like the wheel of time. Souls come and go… come and go…"

"The greatest answers lie not in knowing, but in becoming," Prajothi responded.

Rahasi knew this was a distracted answer. She once again stuck to the same question, she knew this was a test of her one-pointedness. She was determined. She asked once again, "Who is this feminine? What makes her so powerful?"

Prajothi exhaled a slow, deep breath. The air around them grew thick, charged with something ancient.

"This is the secret of all secrets," she said, her voice like the echo of a forgotten past.

She glanced at her brows and ascertained she was ready to receive the key — "The realm has now been opened by Kalyan's dream."

Rahasi's eyes sharpened. "Realm? What realm?"

Prajothi did not answer directly. "It should not be spoken but only experienced," she conveyed telepathically. She shifted her gaze ever so slightly towards the water. The fishes that had been circling playfully now moved with intent.

They began to dance, following her eye movements. It was breathtaking and magical.

Prajothi was communicating that which should not be spoken through her eye movements. Her gaze reflected onto the water, guiding the fishes to form symbols with their movements. They danced gracefully in the water, their bodies shimmering and weaving sacred patterns. Rahasi watched in awe, understanding that these were not mere shapes, but messages conveyed through the dance of the fish, a silent language of the universe itself.

Their tiny bodies shimmered, forming shapes in the rippling water. Rahasi's heart pounded as she saw the pattern they created—sacred symbols that she had learned from her tribe. The familiar symbols, now appearing in the water, resonated deeply within her, as though the universe itself was speaking to her in a language older than time.

Prajothi's voice came one last time, carrying the weight of finality. "Once you know the secret of all secrets, you are no longer who you are."

Rahasi listened. Something in her wanted to swim deeper. She again accessed her inner worlds.

Still, deep in meditation, Rahasi tapped into every hidden thread within Prajothi's words, the patterns made by the fishes — holding onto the sounds to be precise. The message had been cryptic, yet layered with undeniable truth.

Her breath slowed. Her body remained still. But within her, a tempest was awakening.

She turned inward, tapping into the dormant energy coiled at the base of her spine—the sacred Kundalini. She willed it to rise, summoning it like an ancient fire from the depths of her being. The energy surged, slithering upward, burning through every knot of hesitation, every illusion of self. Her vision zoomed very slowly.

Like fire consuming dry wood, the energy blazed through her, igniting every nerve in her body. And then, she saw it.

She was no longer in the cave. No longer in her body. She had entered Kalyan's dream.

She saw what he had seen.
A field of endless darkness stretched before her, yet it was not void—it was charged, alive with massive supersonic energy. The planets moved in their eternal dance, their orbits glowing with unseen forces. Beyond them, beyond even the known edges of the cosmos, she saw Her — A COSMIC GODDESS. Radiant and ethereal, the very embodiment of the universe's untold mysteries. Her presence was vast, like the stars themselves, yet impossibly close, filling Rahasi's mind with a profound sense of awe and reverence. The goddess seemed to pulse with an energy that transcended time and

space, her form ever-shifting, as though she was both everywhere and nowhere at once. Rahasi felt the connection deep within her soul, as if the goddess was awakening something ancient and powerful inside her with innumerable faces, hands, and a beauty surmounting billions of stars and worlds spinning around.

She was white as a star, radiant as the first dawn. Her form was too vast to be contained by a single vision—she was here, there, everywhere. As Rahasi tried to grasp Her presence, the vision suddenly shifted. She was floating following Kalyan's dream patterns. Next her vision changed.

The graveyard.

A river ran beside it, its waters thick with forgotten whispers. The sky was restless, torn apart by flashes of lightning. And there—standing at the edge of the grave—was a hooded figure.

Rahasi watched in silent horror as the figure bent forward, its shadow stretching unnaturally. It reached down and snatched the Rudraksha from Kalyan's body. Then, with an eerie fluidity, it turned and disappeared—into the waters.

The vision pulled her deeper.

She saw Kalyan, standing at the grave where he had fallen unconscious. He was awake now. The roaring wind tried to shake him, but he stood firm. The lightning struck again, illuminating the grave.

Ancient letters glowed on the stone.

She leaned closer.

And then—she saw it — K A L K H A M.

KALKHAM

The moment she saw the word, something deep within her broke open. She did not know what it meant. But she felt it. A word older than language. A sound heavier than existence itself.

The very air around her vibrated. The two worlds had collided.

An overwhelming force rushed into her. The energy was not hers, not his—it was Everything. The influx of power fused with her spine, expanding beyond her body, beyond her identity.

She was no longer Rahasi.

She was no longer just a woman, nor a seeker.

She had become a Force.

The cave seemed to expand and contract in a single breath. Rahasi felt as though her very identity was slipping through her fingers.

Was she ready to step beyond herself?

Was she ready to see what lay beyond the veil?

The air grew still. The symbol in the water shimmered.

And Rahasi knew—there was no turning back.

To be continued…

"The moment you realize everything, you lose everything.
And by losing 'that moment', you not only win,
but transform into a force."

"Some battles are won by winning,
some by losing,
and others by **'just be**' ing in the moment." ~Kalkham

KALKHAM SERIES

A thrilling mythical mystery revolves around Kal,
who chooses a human life to accomplish a secret
mission. To fulfill his complex journey, he inherits
a secret wisdom found only from KALKHAM space
(a universe where seven races of human beings
were prototyped and deployed to planet Earth).

He unexpectedly meets the creator of a parallel
universe, who makes stars and installs illusions
into the minds of all species on earth.

Kal is informed on his inability to complete
his journey on Earth without a female energy.
Is this a trap?

Khamyaka enters Earth from a 7th-dimensional
space and realizes that there is a Naga governing
a secret portal. Why is this portal so closely
guarded?

She finds a big flaw in Kal's strategy. Why
did destiny link these two mortals here, in this
infinite structure?

The incarnate of the sun has a mission to complete...
KALKHAM becomes aware of a new serious situation.
TIME should not stop on earth, but...

ABOUT THE AUTHOR

Venkatesh Nagarajan is the author of the Kalkham series.

Kalkham originated from a deep-rooted thought process and was built purely on the author's imagination, experiences, and research.

The inspiration for this work comes from Veda Vyas and the mighty generations of seers whose wisdom has deeply influenced his thoughts in creating this series.

Want to share your thoughts with the author?
Visit the official website: www.kalkham.com